A[...]

Journey
to Be
Liked

Alfred's Journey to Be Liked

And 10 Simple Rules to Get Him There

A Novel By

Jill Ebstein

This is a work of fiction. Names, events, and incidents are purely the product of the author's imagination.

FIRST EDITION 2023
ISBN: 978-0-9962674-6-5
eBook ISBN: 978-0-9962674-7-2

To all those who encouraged me
and gave me feedback and support—
family, friends, readers, and loyal pets.

Our coaches come in all shapes and sizes,
and we need them all.

Table of Contents

Foreword 11

Part 1 17

Prologue 19

Finding a Coach 21

Explaining Alfred 23

Chunk 1: Alfred and Coach Meet 27

Chunk 2: Don't Be a Know-Betterer 35

Chunk 3: Walking in Someone Else's Shoes 41

Chunk 4: Explaining a Generous Spirit to Alfred 47

Chunk 5: My Lunchroom Then and Now—
A Composition for Coach 53

Chunk 6: Why Ha-Ha Matters 57

Chunk 7: A Review Before Winter Break 65

Chunk 8: Can a Backtrack Be a ZigZag? 73

Chunk 9: Alfred Faces His Fears—Game On! 79

Chunk 10: Wanna Join Grand Masters? 85

Chunk 11: Alfred Struggles with a Math Problem 91

Chunk 12: Alfred Learns He Can Be a 5-Tool Player 99

Chunk 13: Alfred Begins to Identify His Five Tools 105

Chunk 14: Note to Self: Me as a 5-Tool-Player 111

Chunk 15: Hearing the Unspoken 117

Chunk 16: Refresh, Reset, Timeout. 123

Chunk 17: An Unexpected Request Stumps Alfred 129

Chunk 18: Getting to "Yes". 137

Chunk 19: Popposites—Lessons of Another Kind 143

Chunk 20: Building Culture One Joke at a Time 149

Chunk 21: Are There Some Soho Globs in the House? 155

Part 2 161

Chunk 22: Talking to Yourself 163

Chunk 23: A Heart-to-Heart with Mom. 169

Chapter 24: The Glass Half-Full. 175

Chunk 25: All Moms are Alike—or Are They? 183

Chunk 26: What's in a Color? (Language Arts Assignment #5)
An Essay by Alfred. . . . . , , , 189

Chunk 27: Understanding Another Side 191

Chunk 28: Alfred and Joey Talk Dogs 197

Chunk 29: Float Like a Butterfly:
Alfred Chooses His Style. 203

Chunk 30: Assumptions Gone Wild. 209

Chunk 31: It's Granny Time. 217

Chunk 32: Back in Coach's Saddle 223

Chunk 33: Straight Talk and Discovery. 231

Chunk 34: Blue Sky Abounds. 239

Chunk 35: Coach and Hannah Explore Being Happy 247

Chunk 36: Change is in the Air 253

Chunk 37: Click Your Heels Three Times. 261

Chunk 38: The Big Reveal or
The Question I Never Asked Until I Did 267

Chunk 39: I've Got the Moody Blues. 277

Chunk 40: A No-Goodbye Goodbye 283

Chunk 41: A Good Walk Made Great 291

The Epilogue. 297

How Alfred's Journey to Be Liked Spoke to My Son and Me
By Scot Butwell 301

Alfred's Journey to Be Liked
Ten Simple Rules to Help Get Him There 307

An Interview with Jill Ebstein
By Jill Ebstein 315

Alfred's Journey to Be Liked Study Guide Questions. 323

Foreword

*B*efore I begin writing, I usually spend time considering what I want to write and then plan out its loose trajectory. It's how I stay on track and focused. My creation of Alfred was nothing like that. We were in the middle of a pandemic, and I had discovered Medium, a platform for anyone who wants to write something that others will potentially read. "Potentially" because there are somewhere between eighty-five and one hundred million users on the platform, so being read is a lot like the fantasies authors write about.

I observed writers complaining about wanting more claps (a Medium feature of approval) and, in general, wishing they could be better liked. For some reason, I started thinking about middle-school behavior, and my imagination took me to the creation of a young boy who was also not sufficiently liked, only he didn't seem to care. I wondered what it would feel like to be him. I gave this fictional boy a name—Alfred—and wrote my first piece.

Before I knew it, I had inhabited Alfred's world and spun a whole story. Much of my inspiration came from a growing concern that our social skills were atrophying during Covid. Everything seemed like day-old porridge that was cold and tasteless, and it made us angry and hard to be around. Alfred became my think tank for how to rebuild stronger social muscles. Here was a loveable, quirky young teen who liked to play chess, solve hard math problems, and watch Naruto while eating his favorite Soho Glob cookies.

I woke up every morning thinking about Alfred and the challenges he would face on that particular day. Soon, I discovered that he had a reserved and equally quirky mom who brought Alfred wisdom, love, and certitude, albeit delivered dryly. Next, I found Coach, whose job was to help Alfred get a bead (a baseball term because Alfred loves baseball) on building a more connected social life. Coach would need a quiet demeanor and an inventive way to help a smart teen see things for himself.

My writing ship had sailed into unchartered waters as I also broke with some writing conventions. Much of the book would happen through dialogue, and its chapters would be in chunks. The use of dialogue was a very efficient means of telling the story and would accommodate readers' short attention spans. Chunks reinforced that breaking things down into small pieces is the easiest way to solve seemingly intractable problems.

I found other ways to surprise and, maybe, confuse the reader. I introduced some new language. Hence "know-betterers" and "ppoposites" become phrases that play an important role in telling Alfred's story. Alfred and Coach's language soon became mine and eventually the language of my friends and family as we would bemoan the know-betterers in our lives.

Readers will discover that there is very little physical description of Alfred or his world. No sunsets are described, and you have no idea what Alfred might be wearing on a given day or even what he looks like. In that sense, I've provided a blank canvas where readers can imagine Alfred any way they want.

But this I know: You will hear Alfred's unmistakable voice—how he sounds and thinks. And that is the stamp I want readers to remember. His sound is heartwarming and enlightening—a "twofer," as Alfred would say.

It is predictable that I would be drawn to Alfred's voice. In my day job, I capture the "voice of the customer" for clients who want to know how customers think about a range of things. It means that I have to listen hard for unspoken words—feelings that people are either hesitant to articulate or don't know much about but still reside within them. Coach helps Alfred hear the unspoken word and introduces him to many other social necessities.

I then asked "my customers," beta readers whose backgrounds span disciplines—teachers, parents, therapists, and young adults—to read *Alfred's Journey to Be Liked* and provide feedback. I needed to hear their voices, which proved extremely helpful in making this a better book. While many questions and observations were offered, I learned three things in particular from my feedback loop.

Number 1: Alfred is neurodivergent.

I did not intend to create a neurodivergent character, and I resisted any labels that might identify Alfred as such. We have grown to a place in our culture where labels equate to overly simplistic thinking. But I also respected the trained eyes of my therapist readers. I was often asked, "Who in your world is neurodivergent?" and my answer was, "Aren't we all?"

From there, a conversation might ensue where I was coached not to minimize the challenges of truly neurodivergent people, nor was I to try and "normalize" them. I wasn't trying to normalize anyone, but I was trying to help Alfred build a more connected world. His mom (yes, also my creation) felt he'd be happier with "a circle of friends" as she knew all too well about the pain of growing up lonely.

Because of the reader-therapists' feedback and the confusion of other readers who often asked, "Is Alfred on the spectrum?" I decided that I needed to declare Alfred neurodivergent. It felt as if I were coming out of a closet that I'd never thought existed. Still, as one reader shared, "I will be able to focus more on the story now that I know."

So for the love of my readers and my respect for the neurodivergent community, who may not want to be lumped in with everyone else as "quirky" because it shortchanges their challenges, I have accepted that Alfred is neurodivergent. I will also add a P.S. that some of what challenges Alfred challenges us, too. In that way, Coach's words might help us all.

Number 2: My readers are parents, teachers, and mentors. Another question I was often asked was, "Who is the reader?" Initially, I didn't know, and I naively assumed that *Alfred's Journey to Be Liked* could be a "family read." I then learned from industry experts that family reads, such as *Harry Potter* and *To Kill a Mockingbird,* do not constitute an actual book category, and only a few rare books have filled that hallowed territory over time. It would be the equivalent of being a singer who wants to perform opera at the Met. Beverly Sills earned her way to that spot.

I learned that even though I paid young adults, getting them to read it was a tough slog. By and large, kids prefer more plot-driven stories, speculative fiction, or at least books with some graphics. The combination of not having "family read" as an available category and learning that kids didn't truly enjoy the book enabled me to identify my audience. I had received significant positive feedback from adult readers, even to the point of their asking me what lay ahead for Alfred. They, in fact, cared about him.

So now I know that my readers are adults who bear the challenge and opportunity of helping those who are younger become more socially mature. This translates to parents, relatives, teachers, mentors, coaches, and counselors. It is a work of fiction written by someone who is not a therapist and is devoid of clinical knowledge. I am a mom who, at best, hopes to offer homespun practical ideas that might be useful for getting a conversation started around the dinner table.

Number 3: Alfred's journey is aspirational and not meant to be a realistic portrayal of one year of growth.

My reader-therapists strongly felt that Alfred's progress happened at an unrealistic pace. I equated their comments to watching car commercials in which a stunt driver is speeding through the mountainous terrain to show how well the car handles. On the bottom of the screen is a disclaimer that tells us we are seeing a professional driver and that this should not be tried by the rest of us.

Actually, Alfred's lessons *should* be tried by the rest of us, but we shouldn't expect the learning to happen as readily. In some ways, I've idealized a process and maybe even created a modern-day parable. Coach and Alfred's interactions guide the reader toward a code of moral behavior: "Walk in someone else's shoes," "Don't be a know-betterer," "Soft squishy things matter too," and "Face your fears," for example. But the driver and the car are fiction, which, I hope, we can learn from—at a pace that suits us as individuals.

Changing our behavior, how we look at the world, and where we derive our meaning are full of complexities. Everything takes time in a world that doesn't seem to offer much of it. I do not want to set up readers and their loved ones for disappointment if they aren't able to quickly replicate Alfred's progress. His is a metaphorical school year.

So I offer you this visual metaphor as you begin reading about Alfred's journey. Consider a sweater you might wish to unravel. Where do you start? My answer is that you pick a thread—any thread—and pull. It will happen as it happens, and eventually, you might have a skein with which you can begin again.

More than anything, I hope Alfred's journey spawns some great conversations. What are my five tools? Can I be a culture builder? Hear the unspoken? Find my generosity? Laugh either as a creator or appreciator of humor because now I know that both matter? As we emerge from the dark days of Covid, can this book serve as a kind of social boot camp to remind us of what we may have forgotten?

Let the conversations start…

P.S., Check out Scot Butwell's piece at the end of this book on his experience in sharing *Alfred's Journey to Be Liked* with his son. His story is my objective.

Part 1

Prologue

A mom and her son are on the sofa watching another *Friends* episode. They do this almost every night. Her son enjoys his favorite cookie—Soho Globs—while they watch. His mom makes these cookies every Sunday. On some nights, they finish the evening with a game of chess, and then the son is off to bed.

The mom now has the rest of the evening to herself. She has started watching *West Wing*. She loves the characters, the story, the relationships, and the resolution. There is just enough intrigue and personal touch to leave her feeling satisfied as she heads off to bed herself.

Then, one night, she is watching an episode where her reaction is so strong that it leaves her wondering. In this episode, it is Christmas time, and a character named Josh is experiencing significant stress that his boss, Leo, recognizes as needing attention. Leo persists in convincing Josh to speak with someone though Josh doesn't see the need.

At the end of a very long visit between Josh and a therapist, a diagnosis is made with suggested follow-up. As Josh leaves the office, Leo is sitting in a nearby chair, waiting for Josh to emerge.

Josh is surprised that Leo has waited around for him. And then Leo explains why he is sitting there, using a parable that is so moving that the mom cannot help but repeat it over and over again in her mind:

A guy is walking down the street when he falls down a steep hole that he can't get out of. He yells for someone to hear him. "Hey you, can you help me out?" A doctor passing by hears him and writes a prescription, throws it down the hole, and moves on. After that, a priest passes by, and again, the guy who is still stuck down below shouts out, "Hey Father, can you help me out?" The priest writes out a prayer, throws it down the hole, and then moves on. Finally, a friend is walking by, and the guy in the hole recognizes him. He calls out, "Hey Joe can you help me out?" The friend quickly descends into the hole. Now, the guy who asked for help says, "Joe, are you stupid? Now we're both stuck down here." The friend replies, "Yeah, but I've been down here before, and I know the way out."

The mom cannot help wondering about her draw to this story. She goes to sleep, and when she wakes up, she understands. It is personal. Her son, Alfred, is also stuck in a hole. Yes, Alfred has a fine chess game, a love of math, total immersion into baseball stats, and her—baker of cookies, TV companion, and chess player. But Alfred has no friends. She understands that the man stuck in the hole—that *West Wing* moment of poignancy—could just as well be about Alfred.

She knows that hole. So, what is she to do? Does she descend into this hole and revisit old pains? If she does, will she get out?

What should she do to help Alfred?

Finding a Coach

*I*t was always going to be tough. There was no partner to off-load Alfred to when she got tired. Playing chess was great, but it could only take them so far. Same thing for watching *Friends* or doing a simultaneous book read as when Harry Potter came out.

She couldn't help but wonder whether there had been a pattern baked into her life. Her mom had raised her largely as a single parent, though there were moments when her dad was around. At least her mom knew of the loneliness and worry of being the only parent.

Fortunately, her mom had been helpful, but she, too, had her demons. Widowed too young, a love that proved too elusive a times, a daughter that was smart but lacked friends. Again, she thought, a repeating pattern of sorts.

It was time to break the pattern. She would find just the right kind of person that could help Alfred. With no men in Alfred's life, mom would try to find a kind and thoughtful male coach. He would need to be low-key. He would need to be patient. Alfred did not adjust to change well. The coach she would find would need to understand that he was just one piece of a larger puzzle—a puzzle with odd colors and pieces that didn't fit so well together. But over time, "Coach," as she began to think of him, could help Alfred create his own rich tapestry. Or, given it was Alfred, his own "table of numbers" that helped him make sense of his world.

"There," she thought. "We've moved from puzzle to a tapestry to maybe numbers if needed." Just expanding the vocabulary to describe Alfred's world was a start.

She would ask around. She wasn't in a rush, but she would persist until she found the right fit. Then she would explain to Alfred why this was important. "Coach," as she now thought of him, wouldn't ask too much of Alfred. He would be of help in a way that Alfred couldn't realize until much later.

She was sure that Alfred would resist, but she would rely upon Alfred's immense trust in her. She might even barter with him for more nightly chess games if need be. She could still beat Alfred, but one day, he would be better, and chess as a bargaining chip wouldn't be available.

She believed that Alfred would grow to value aspects of life that weren't just about numbers, just about things he could quantify. Maybe, he'd even stop asking that question, "On a scale of one to ten, low to high, how would you rate…."

Mom held hope that one fine day Alfred would see her decision to bring Coach into their lives as one gigantically strategic chess move—many steps ahead and critical in setting up the win.

It would be good. She was ready for good.

Explaining Alfred

Alfred's mom thought about how she would explain "Alfred" when the time came. She recalled her many conversations with Alfred's teacher, Ms. Baker. She had wanted to know whether Alfred had any friends. Did he seem engaged at school? Did Alfred look happy? She couldn't help but worry whether Alfred "belonged," and if not, what could they do?

Ms. Baker had been helpful. She always was. She understood Alfred for all his good and all his quirky ways. Alfred's mom could still hear Ms. Baker's words when she asked, "Eleanor, is it you who worries about Alfred, or does Alfred worry about Alfred?"

Eleanor knew the answer. She worried about Alfred. When her pediatrician had suggested that "Alfred might be on the spectrum," Eleanor went straight to Google to learn what that meant. The more she read, the better she understood both herself and Alfred. They were, by design, very literal. They liked alone time. They would never be the life of the party. For them, the party was playing chess and eating popcorn.

She had found comfort in the pediatrician's use of the word

"might." How would they know? Were there degrees of behavior? Would it change the course of Alfred's life? For all these questions and more, the pediatrician shared that yes, there were degrees, and at least as Alfred was concerned, if he was on the spectrum, he seemed to be functioning at a high level. He went to school, did well, had interests that he truly enjoyed, could talk to people as needed, and seemed overall happy.

"I tell you this, just so you are aware, in case it becomes a challenge as Alfred matures. It is the kind of thing I'd keep my eye on but not get too, too focused on."

All this made sense, but then Eleanor did what she usually did when she felt nervous. She went to her mom. Her mom was smart, thoughtful, and had been around the block. Plus, she was their biggest champion.

"Ellie," her mom said, "You weren't so easy either, but look how you turned out. I wouldn't worry too much. Anyway, you and Alfred are a lot alike. If it makes you feel better, find someone who can work with Alfred. They do so much more these days than when you were growing up. But you'll see. Alfred will be fine. Even better than fine. He'll be great. By the way, I think he's great now."

It took Eleanor three months until she found just the right guy. Tom had a quiet presence. He didn't say much, but every word counted. When she told Tom about Alfred—that he'd be resistant, that he was very literal, that he wouldn't see the point in working on anything that seemed "soft" like interpersonal skills—Tom just shook his head with a knowing kind of nod.

"I've been there before. I think we can give it a go and see how it lands."

Eleanor waited for Tom to elaborate, but he didn't. Instead, they shared an awkward silence. Then, to mitigate the pain of the moment, they both started to talk, and then they simultaneously stopped. More awkwardness, and then laughter.

"Well, you've got me laughing, so that's a good sign. Ok, I'll start, Tom. Let's give it a go, as you say. But I'd like to refer to you as 'Coach.' For one thing, it's what you'll be doing. And for another, Alfred has a hard time remembering names."

Tom smiled. "I like Coach better anyway. It could become my new moniker. I should have thought of it myself."

And that was that. All was set. Next week would be Coach and Alfred's first meeting. It was now time for fate to take its course. Eleanor had done her job.

Chunk 1:

Alfred and Coach Meet

Alfred's mom succeeded in convincing Alfred to give Coach a try. She had to explain that a few more friends would make Alfred's life "richer." Oh, how she loved that word. "Richer" wasn't about money or about the very chocolatey Soho Globs she made Alfred weekly. It was about adding more dimension to what otherwise seemed like a skinny and narrow kind of life.

"I'm not saying that you haven't tried to make friends, Alfred, but Coach can maybe be of help. What do we have to lose?" Alfred was about to say, "I have what I need," but then he took another glance at his mom. He liked pleasing her, and who knows? Maybe she was right, and so Alfred reluctantly agreed.

She explained to Alfred that she had done her homework and had found just the right guy—low key, experienced with kids, and very approachable. At least, those were her impressions based on their phone call, one meeting, and the series of questions she had asked.

"How will I know if this will work?" Alfred's mom remembered asking.

"Well, it will take us some time to sort through but eventually we—and by 'we' I mean, you, me and Alfred—will know. It will be as plain as the nose on your face."

Her face must have given her up because she looked doubtful. Even worried.

Then Coach added, "I'm reading your face, and I see angst. I truly believe that we can manage the experience so that it won't be overwhelming to Alfred. I will chunk things into pieces so that it won't feel so big. We'll see how it goes."

That was good enough, and she explained all of this to Alfred. "Your first meeting with Coach will be on Monday. We'll take it one step at a time and see what you think." She was careful to say "meeting" and not "session" because "session" sounded too cold and clinical.

Alfred's response was predictable. He wasn't happy. "On Monday? Mondays are usually awful days to start something. And you know that I have statistics to back this up. Also, does this guy really go by the name 'Coach'? That sounds so generic to me."

Hearing the word "generic" from her fourteen-year-old son made her laugh. He could remember sophisticated words but not people's names. She immediately shot back,

"Alfred, you always have statistics in your back pocket, and some of them are even helpful. But not in this case. And I call him 'Coach' because that is what he will be doing, and names can be hard to remember. But if you prefer, you can call him by his name, which is Tom."

Alfred shrugged in resignation. He wasn't happy, but he wasn't going to win this one. Maybe he could take his frustration out during their nightly game of chess. "I'll call him 'Coach' because it is easier. We'll see if he lives up to his name. And just so you know, I am seeing a single digit number of meetings—so less than ten."

This made Alfred's mom chuckle. It always came back to numbers. That's who Alfred was.

But she couldn't resist adding, "Alfred, just promise me you will be open-minded."

Here's how Alfred and Coach's first session went. First, Alfred stared at Coach. Coach smiled. He let the moment of awkwardness sink in. After a minute of silence, Coach decided he would start.

Coach: Hello Alfred. I've heard a little about you, and I am glad to meet you.

Silence, again. Coach counted to fifteen in his head, and just as he got ready to say something, Alfred began.

Alfred: I'm told I can call you 'Coach.' So, Coach, I don't need much — just a friend or two to text with, trade some music picks with, and maybe even talk sports. I told my mom that I am seeing a single-digit number of meetings with you.

Coach: Ok. I only want to help you where I can be of help. So, tell me, what happens when you meet someone that you'd like to be friends with?

Alfred: I ask them what things they like. It could be sports, video games...podcasts. Things like that. When they tell me, I usually can speak about whatever they like.

Coach: What do you mean "speak about"? Do you ask them why they like something? Or do you just rattle off what you know? What exactly do you do?

Alfred: Well, I love numbers. When I am older, I want to make my money in analytics. Don't people say, "Do what you love?" I love data. Most people love data, don't they? That's what I share with the people I might want to be friends with.

Coach: Well, it's great that you love numbers. You just have to be careful not to seem like the smartest person in the room. No one likes that.

Alfred: Even if I am the smartest person in the room?

Coach: Yes, "even if." It's best to let them discover it on their own.

Alfred: That can take a long time—and a lot of patience. Can we go with another tip that can help me? It will be hard for me to hide my smarts, but I can try. I know it's best when people come to discoveries on their own.

Coach: Ok. Here's another. How good are you at listening?

Alfred: Define listening.

Coach: When a potential friend says something, are you thinking about your response, or are you trying to understand how they come at their world?

Alfred: Doesn't everyone think about their response? That is how I make sure I am prepared. No one likes to be caught off guard. I thought I was doing a good thing.

Coach: It is true that being prepared is a good thing. But when someone is talking, it's better to really hear that person. Even better would be to take a few minutes before you respond. You know, "Think before you speak."

Alfred: That seems like a hard one, too. Can you give me another tip? So far, you want me to hide my smarts and really listen before I speak. I need something easier. My mom says that it's important to build confidence. So, I think you need to give me something that will do that. Then, as I understand it, more confidence equals more friends.

Coach: Yes, I see your point. And by the way, no one said that making new friends would be easy. Ok, here is one more tip. People like to talk about themselves. Do you ask questions? Do you let them talk? Also, if you refer to them by name, that helps. People love to hear their name.

Alfred: That seems doable. Am I allowed to write their name down—maybe on my hand—to help me remember? And are there better questions to ask than others?

Coach: Wait! You can remember numbers and statistics, but names are hard for you?

Alfred: Yes. Is that unusual? Numbers tell a story. Names just identify a person.

Coach: I think I am beginning to see our challenge. Ok, Alfred, treat people like they are a number—a statistic. Then you will remember them, find them interesting, and figure out what questions to ask. Your curiosity will lead you.

Alfred: Now that's great coaching. Maybe calling you 'Coach' will actually fit. With that last tip, it's possible that my chance of making some new friends just doubled.

Coach and Alfred's mom talk afterward. Coach begins.
"I know you want to call me 'Coach.' We never addressed what I should call you."

Alfred's mom smiles. "I think of myself as 'Alfred's mom.' Some people call me by my name, Eleanor. My mom calls me 'Ellie' for short. You can pick. But back to Alfred, how big a challenge do we have here?"

"Well," replies Coach, "Our plan needs to rely on Alfred's strength. I think if we treat people like numbers, we can get him there."
Now a big smile breaks out on Eleanor's face.

"Numbers do make the world go round. It makes sense to me. I'll see you next week," she says and then adds as an afterthought, "By the way, I like calling you 'Coach' because I think I will learn from you, too."

With that, it was Coach's turn to smile. "Same time next week, Eleanor?"

"Yes, and can you check in with me after each session? I think it will help all of us. I've known Alfred since the start, obviously, and my mom has said that we are a lot alike. We probably are. I might be able to provide insight."

Coach understood, but he also knew he would have to clear this with Alfred. After all, that was standard practice for someone Alfred's age, no matter how helpful the mom might be. And so, Coach explained, "Eleanor, I need to discuss this with Alfred first. I am sure you could be quite helpful, but I would need Alfred to agree. Let me get back to you, ok?"

With a nod of the head, Eleanor sighed, "Ok," and then she watched Coach head out the door.

Chunk 2:

Don't Be a Know-Betterer

*I*t took no time for Coach to discern Alfred's smarts and his lack of softer skills. What would be the best way to help Alfred? "I'll need patience and time—probably more than the one-digit number of sessions Alfred has limited us to."

Coach thinks back to his confusion. Alfred sounded mature—like an adult. But then Coach could see some of the gaps. He wonders, "Maybe I should follow Alfred's lead and write his age on my hand so that I am careful not to overestimate him?" This thought makes him chuckle.

Alfred's reaction to Coach's explaining that "A person's name is literally their favorite word" seemed particularly noteworthy. That statement felt so odd to Alfred. This would be a good place to start. Then as if to give himself his own pep talk, Coach reminds himself, "Rome wasn't built in a day. Patience will be key."

Now Coach is ready to engage.

Coach: Alfred, how is it going?

Alfred: Not bad. On a scale of one to ten, low to high, my mood is an eight today.

Coach: Well, eight isn't bad. We can't all be ten all the time. Tell me what has improved since last week when we talked.

Alfred: Mostly, I've been working on learning people's names. I write them down on my hand. I've even color-coded them. "Red" is for the names I must learn right away. I've given myself more time for purple names. And no more than five can appear on my hand at any one time.

Coach: Wow, that sounds like a good system. It must be hard to wash off the ink at the end of the night.

Alfred: Well, yeah, but I count to ten for every name I scrub off, and that usually gets me there.

Coach: Ok, are we ready for a new lesson to help you build more friendships?

Alfred: I'm ready. I still have to work on last week's lessons, though. I am having a hard time not treating people like numbers. The thing is, I love numbers, and I love the transitive property. In my mind, treating people like numbers means I love them too. But yes, I am ready.

Coach: This week's lesson is simple. Don't be a know-betterer.

Alfred: What does that mean?

Coach: It means that you shouldn't pass yourself off as someone who always knows better than others.

Alfred: Ok, I am going to ask the same question as I did last time—even if I really do know better?

Coach: Yes, even if.

Alfred: Remind me why.

Coach: Because people don't want to feel like they are at the bottom of the heap. They want to feel as if they know something. And guess what—they usually do. It just might be something different than what you know.

Alfred begins to shift in his chair as he tries to get comfortable. It's not clear whether it is the seat or the idea of not being a know-betterer that causes him to be restless.

Coach: Think of it as a way of showing respect when you hold back how much you know. Even better, think of it as a learning opportunity. Maybe they know something that you haven't yet learned.

Alfred: That's a lot to take in. Can you give me some examples? How do I not be a "know-betterer," as you call it?

Coach: Let's say you are talking sports—one of your favorite topics. You like baseball, right? If someone says that the game of baseball is in trouble because it's too slow, and young kids today aren't playing the game like they used to, how might you respond?

Alfred: Well, that person is mostly right but not completely. I would begin by highlighting how much money MLB lost last year. I would add that the average game takes over three hours despite the league's best efforts to speed it up. I might even discuss how teams in big cities and TV licenses drive the game—and not in a good way.

Coach: And that would be the problem.

Alfred: What—the TV licenses?

Coach: No. Your overall response. Why not take one of those points and turn it into a question? You could ask, "Do you know if MLB lost money last year? Just wondering." Or you could say, "I thought they changed the rules to speed up the game. Do you know if it worked?"

Alfred: Ok, even though I pretty much know the answers to those questions.

Coach: I know you know. But again, we are working on how not to be a know-betterer. This is hard for everyone. Adults need to learn this too. From Netflix picks to politics to how we live life, everyone thinks they know better. They have the code that can help us all.

Alfred: Wow, super cool if what I need to work on is the same thing that my mom needs to work on. For me, your using a baseball analogy is an added plus—a home run, so to speak. So, can you give me one tip to help me not be a know-betterer? And it shouldn't be something that I write on my hand. My hand already has a lot of names on it.

Coach: Ok, I've got a suggestion. I'll share with you what I do. I count to five—in my head, Alfred—before I say something. While I'm counting, I think about whether what I have to say is—how should I put this—"additive." Am I adding to the person's point? Remember—it is still their point.

Alfred: I like the idea of counting to five. It is super helpful for me to use a number to guide me…. (silence)… I just counted to five. Let's leave it there.

Coach: One more thing, Alfred. Your mom would like it if I can touch base with her… you know, let her know how it's going or if she can be in any way helpful. Are you ok with that? This is one instance where you are the boss.

Alfred: (quiet, thinking) Coach, I was counting to five again before answering. My mom is smart. She might help make this whole thing go faster, so yes, you can talk to her afterward. I think if there is something I don't want you to share, I will tell you.

Coach checks in with Alfred's mom after the second session.

"Ok, Alfred said that I can meet with you afterward and keep you in the loop. He is hoping that makes, and here I use Alfred's words, 'This whole thing will go faster.'"

That makes Alfred's mom chuckle. It sounded so "Alfred" to her, and of course, the next thing would be his estimating how much faster it could make the process go.

Coach continues, "We are working on how not to be a know-betterer. It's particularly hard when you really do know better than the people around you."

Now, this idea has Alfred's mom completely intrigued. Coach sees it, and as he begins to wonder why, she smiles and says, "Hmm… I wonder if this lesson is something I could benefit from."

After the Coach counts to five, he says, "Give it some thought. See you next week."

Chunk 3:
Walking in Someone Else's Shoes

*A*lfred is starting to get accustomed to working with Coach to "Build his circle" to borrow his mother's words. Alfred has already learned that it doesn't serve him well to always lead with smarts. He is trying to lead with curiosity. That part comes naturally, but the names? Not so much.

"I am going to do what you suggest," Alfred tells Coach, "But you should know that 'Alfred' is not my favorite word." Coach wonders what Alfred's favorite word is, but he tells himself, "We have bigger fish to fry." Anyway, he figures that Alfred's favorite word will show itself eventually.

Coach: So, Alfred, how's it going?

Alfred: I think I'm making progress. I'm learning people's names and actually using them. I don't need to color-code them on my hands anymore. Also, I'm trying hard not to show people that I know better—even though I usually do. And I've noticed people letting me sit with them at lunch, and they are even using my name, which, by the way, does feel good. You might be right.

Coach: Wonderful. So, I think then we are ready for our next lesson.

Alfred: Shoot.

Coach: Wait. Isn't "shoot" a basketball term? I think you have just gone from your favorite sport of baseball to basketball. Wow—a changeup! Just so you know, in general, coaches like changeups, and I mean that symbolically. We like when people change a habit or pattern. It shows a willingness to be open and explore.

Alfred: I think that's the point of our meetings, right?

Coach: Yes. So back to our focus for today, do you have a favorite book or two?

Alfred: Well, more like ten. I love the *Narnia series*, and *Lord of the Rings*, and of course, all the *Harry Potter* books. Do you want me to keep going?

Coach: No, that's enough. My favorite book as a kid, and still one of mine as an adult, is *To Kill a Mockingbird*. I loved the story and the characters, and Harper Lee's message. Something I read in that book has stuck with me ever since. Have you read the book?

Alfred: Yes. It was required reading. It was pretty good. Sad sometimes. Slow other times. But even still, I liked it.

Coach: What I remember was Atticus telling Scout to try and feel what others are feeling. He tells her to wear other people's shoes.

Alfred: Yes, I remember that. To tell you the truth, I never really understood Atticus's advice. The way I see it, feet are different sizes. Styles are different too. And then you've got the girl versus boy thing. I know that's not how Atticus meant it, but just so you know, I wouldn't be caught dead wearing ballerina slippers or girls' shoes in general.

Coach: So, you are continuing to understand the phrase literally. Try seeing it as a metaphor. Can you guess what Atticus is saying that is actually not about physically wearing someone's shoes?

Alfred: Well, I remember what our teacher said. She said that if I put on someone's shoes, I might be able to see the world through their eyes. I guess we can forget that feet don't see and remember that the shoes are a symbol.

Coach: Exactly. So, what is the benefit of seeing through someone else's eyes?

Alfred: I am sorry to do this, but I am still stuck because I wouldn't actually be walking around because the shoes would probably not fit. I could fall. Whoops! There I go again—being literal.

The room becomes quiet as Alfred and Coach now stare at each other. Coach is trying to figure out how to make his point in a way that Alfred will understand while Alfred is looking down to see what shoes he is wearing.

Alfred: Ok. I'm going to try and give Atticus the benefit here. I will consider wearing others' shoes as a way of understanding people better. If I can do that, I will have upped my game from remembering their name to knowing something about them.

Coach: You've got it! And with this comes other benefits. Maybe you will show more kindness or patience. Maybe you will be slower to criticize. We'll just have to see.

Alfred: Maybe this is how I will be able to stop being a know-betterer. This is the biggest challenge yet of all you've given me.

Coach: Alfred, it's hard for all of us. Adults use the word "empathy" to try and place themselves in someone's shoes. It's about understanding discomfort, pain, and things that make life hard for that person.

Alfred: I liked what you were saying until you got to the pain part. Can we rename your idea? My teacher, Ms. Baker, uses the word "perspective" when we study literature.

Coach: "Perspective" works.

Alfred: Maybe I can use your idea of symbolic shoes in a class assignment. I never told you this, but I like "twofers." So, if I can gain more friends and bring a clever idea to my class, it is what I call a "twofer" which is good.

Coach: That makes sense. One more thing. I still worry that you will fall back into a literal understanding of "wearing someone's shoes." What will you do to remind yourself that it is about "perspective" and not stumbling in a pair of shoes that don't fit?

Alfred: That is a super good question. I can write on my hand. It worked with names. And my hands have space again. I'll just write "symbol."

Coach: Ok. If and when you get stuck—and we all do—my tip for you is to ask questions. Lead with curiosity.

Alfred: I can do that. It might make me seem nicer.

Coach: And, in case you tend to do this, when you ask questions and you get responses, you need to make sure to show that you are "taking it all in." Specifically, do not appear "judgy" or skeptical if that makes sense.

Alfred: It does, but just so you know, you're asking a lot of me.

Coach: I know, but in my short time with you, I can see you are very capable. My assignment for you this week is to apply wearing someone else's symbolic shoes and to report back on how it helped you understand that person better. See you next week.

Alfred: Ok. Who knows—maybe I'll surprise you. Maybe I'll even surprise me.

Coach checks in with Alfred's mom. "Alfred is making good progress, and we are now working on trying to understand how others experience their world. It's what you and I would call empathy, but for Alfred, I use a different expression."

Alfred's mom's curiosity is suddenly piqued. "What are you using?"

"I am leaning on Harper Lee's *To Kill a Mockingbird* where Atticus tells his kids that they need to walk in others' shoes."

Mom smiles. "I love that book, and I know that is something we all need to work on—not just kids. If you are able to help Alfred do this, and you have more than an expression that you use to build that skill, please pass it along. You'd be helping Alfred and me, and my bigger world—kind of a twofer, only actually it's a threefer."

Coach chuckles and mutters quietly, "The apple does not fall far from the tree, and there seem to be apples everywhere." As he walks out the door, he shouts, "You know what would be great? Ask Alfred how he is going about gaining 'perspective'—to use Alfred's word. The two of you learning together would be my perfect twofer. See you next week, Eleanor."

Chunk 4:

Explaining a
Generous Spirit to Alfred

Alfred and Coach are meeting for their fourth session. Alfred has been working hard not to show people how smart he is, and he is continuing to write people's names on his left hand to help him use people's "favorite word." He has added new names when he no longer needs help remembering the old names, and he has since added the word "symbol."

Alfred's mood upon meeting Coach has changed from dread to eager as he looks forward to sharing his update—and a surprise.

Coach: Hey Alfred! How's it going?

Alfred: Good. I am appearing less smart every day. I ask people lots of questions—even when I know the answers. And I never correct them when they're wrong.

Coach: All good! How are you doing in terms of wearing other people's shoes—figuratively, of course?

Alfred: I'm trying and writing the word "symbol" on my hand has helped. I sometimes look at the particular shoes someone is wearing before I make my approach. I think that if I like the shoes, it will help me wear them—even though I won't be really wearing them.

Coach: Do you feel like we are ready for a new challenge?

Alfred: Yes. I'd like another changeup—like we have in baseball. It's funny how baseball has answers for almost everything.

Coach: Well, our changeup will take advantage of the season. 'Tis the season to be jolly,' so I am thinking of things that make us jolly. What makes you jolly, Alfred?

Alfred: Having lunch with my new friends, reading baseball stats, believing the Yankees will fix their team, and definitely tearing into my mom's Soho Globs—the best cookies ever. Oh, and at the end of our session, I have something to share that I think will make you jolly, but let's save that for the end.

Coach: Ok, then. I like surprises. But back to today, I am thinking about generosity—how we give to others, which is timely given the holidays. Is there an element of giving in the things you just mentioned that makes you happy?

Alfred: Definitely. Having a better experience in the lunchroom with people who seem to want me at their table makes me happy. When I hear, "Hey, Alfred, care to join us?" I think you are right. My name might be my favorite word. And whether they really want me at their table, or are just being nice, or maybe need help with their math, it doesn't matter. It feels "generous" to me—to use your word.

Coach: Wow, I like that. What used to happen in the lunchroom?

Alfred: Well, that's the surprise I was going to wait and share at the end, but now it's a surprise for both of us because I am giving it now—not later. I wrote something about my lunchroom experience. Until recently, people didn't know my name or ask me to join them. But that has changed. Here—you can read this later *(handing Coach a document)*.

Coach: I can't wait to read this. Thank you. I am so glad to see some tangible progress that maybe helps you feel that you are really gaining friendship skills.

Alfred: Yes, that part is good. Lunch is a happier place for me. But just so you know, we are not wearing each other's shoes yet. Although if we do, I know whose shoes I am going for first.

Coach: Alfred, you are sounding literal again. But let's return to the topic of generosity and talk about when your mom makes your favorite Soho Globs. What do you give her back?

Alfred: Sometimes, a hug. To be honest, it's a forced hug. I don't really like hugging. Sometimes I agree to watch a show with her. She likes sappy stuff, but I watch it anyway.

Coach: With your friends and your mom, these gifts don't involve money, right?

Alfred: Right. I don't really have much money.

Coach: Which leads me to today's topic. If I use the term "generous spirit," does that mean anything to you?

Alfred: Not a thing... spirits aren't real or generous. They are ghosts that have even less money than me.

Coach: So, we are back to the issue of being literal again.

Alfred: I tend to do that—about as much as you tend to like figurative stuff. I am just curious—are you the kind of person who doesn't like numbers?

Coach: No, I like numbers, but they don't always get me where I need to go. Let's return to the term "generous spirit." It's about finding a way to give of yourself. Not cash, not things, nothing you can touch—unless it is a hug or a hand.

Alfred: Ok, so if I give my friends help with math, does that count?

Coach: Yes

Alfred: And if I tell my mom about something special she did or some advice that she gave me that was helpful, does that count?

Coach: Yes

Alfred: So, it sounds like "generous spirit" just means being a nice person. Maybe for the holidays, I can add a little extra—like math help plus looking at a science assignment.

Coach: Sure

Alfred: Ok, we're good. I would just rename the topic to "generous person." "Spirit" is too confusing.

Coach: I understand how it confuses you, and there is only so much you can write on your hand to keep it straight. Anyway, I have your assignment for next week. I need two examples where someone was generous to you and two instances where you were generous back.

Alfred: I can do that as long as it doesn't involve making me sing or listen to my mom sing. I also don't want to have to share my Soho Globs with friends if I can avoid that. I also don't want to fake a laugh at something not funny. I don't do that well.

Coach: Alfred, whatever you do needs to be genuine. You'll figure it out. And Alfred, thanks for this wonderful surprise. I am really looking forward to reading what you wrote.

Alfred: When you read this, just remember that I am better with numbers than words.

Coach: I hear you. I will be reading for sentiment, not artistry.

Coach proceeds to check in on Alfred's mom. "Look for Alfred showing you that he has a generous spirit," Coach says.

"If it's a spirit, will I know it when I see it?" mom asks. She adds,

"Spirits are supposed to be invisible."

Coach responds as he walks out, "Well, I hear your Soho Globs are literally the best, so if you could, be a generous spirit and send a few globs my way…."

Chunk 5:

My Lunchroom Then and Now—
A Composition for Coach

*H*ere is what my lunchroom looks like to me—then and now. Thanks to Coach, the "now" is much better.

At my school, when you walk into the lunchroom, you see ten long tables, in two rows of five. Each table has benches that can seat twelve people comfortably, but fourteen if you squeeze in. Those numbers were never relevant to me—and I love numbers—because I was never trying to squeeze into any group.

My Lunchroom Then

There is always one table that has a few random kids sitting in odd places around the table. That's where I sit—or sat. One person is at the end of the bench, one in the middle, and a few people sit catty-corner. We're spread out so that we can minimize how much we talk to each other.

We are happy to be eating our lunch in quiet. Carrying on a conversation is hard work and feels awkward for us. So instead, we read our book, or in my case, I am often trying to slay a difficult math dragon. That's how I refer to a stubborn math problem.

My lunchroom experience has changed recently. Even though I was pretty happy to have the lunchroom experience I just described—sitting at a table with a few quiet kids—my mom was dead set on me expanding my circle. That's why I said "ok" to Coach, thinking it would be a few meetings and I'd be done.

When Coach told me that I needed to start by learning people's names, I was doubtful that would make a difference. I listened because, I guess, they don't call him "Coach" for nothing. Well, it turns out Coach was right, and my world has started to change.

A few weeks ago, I was sitting at my corner of the table, when I noticed a person sitting four feet away reading what seemed like a chess book. "Well," I said to myself, "Maybe we have something in common." I like chess.

I ask this boy his name, and he told me it was Mitchell. We started talking about chess, and lunch really did seem a little more fun. I wrote his name on my hand so that I wouldn't forget it.

I used this experience to build some momentum. In baseball and other sports, building momentum is very important, and the same is true with lunchtime. After talking to Mitchell, when I saw an opportunity to speak with someone, I would be brave and ask their name. If I thought I would like them, I wrote the name down on my hand when they weren't looking.

Then last week, I heard some kids at a packed table arguing

about the answer to a math problem. They were sure that they were right and that the teacher had gotten it wrong.

When I heard, "And she marked my answer wrong!" in a loud voice and quite irritated, my curiosity got the best of me. I shyly went up and asked if they could share the problem. I told them that I loved math and maybe I could be of help. At the very least, I'd have my curiosity solved.

Then they told me the problem—and it was geometry, which is my favorite. I saw right away that the teacher was right. So instead of explaining the correct answer, I tried to understand how they saw the problem. This proved much harder for me than simply answering it right. By the end, they started to see that maybe they really did make mistake. I later told my mom, "Mission accomplished." I helped (I think) and learned a few names.

My Lunchroom Now

Now I have two tables to choose from when I go into the lunchroom. There is the table I sat at before with kids who are quiet, and there is the table of loud conversation. One table has five or so kids. The other has twelve to fourteen. I have four or five names scrawled on my hand to help me remember the names of kids at the noisy table. Lunch has become much busier for me.

More often, I sit at the table packed with kids. Sometimes, I am given homework problems to solve, which I am happy to do because they are, after all, becoming my friends. Sometimes, though, I just want the quiet and the space of the other table, so I can give myself a break. I tell the kids at the noisy table that I have a headache and that I need some quiet. It's not exactly true, but I think they understand that better than "I need my space."

It's been five weeks since my first conversation with Coach, but lunch is hugely better. Sometimes, I ask Mitchell to join me at the noisy, crowded table. He doesn't like to, but he will because I am persistent. He knows that on some days, I just really need someone who gets me. Other days, I might end up back at the quiet table where I feel very at home. My mom says that it's ok.

Actually, my mom says, and here I quote, "We need to celebrate ourselves in all our splendor." "Splendor" sounds like a big word and her thought is a big one, but I just translate it to mean that sitting at either lunch table is fine. Because we are allowed to be splendid—or exercise splendor—or whatever.

You get the idea.

Chunk 6:

Why Ha-Ha Matters

*F*or Coach, last week felt like significant progress. Alfred was translating Coach's words into something he could understand. "Generosity of spirit" became "being a nice person." Even better, Alfred chose to write something for Coach that explained how lunchtime was now different.

Coach is now wondering how much he can pack into their once-a-week sessions—especially if he is limited by a single-digit number of visits. He doesn't want to overload Alfred, and he also doesn't want to slow down progress. Mostly, he doesn't know how many sessions they will really have.

Coach thinks he has figured out just the thing.

Coach: Hey Alfred. How's it going?

Alfred: Pretty good. I did my assignment, so I think you'll be happy.

Coach: Great. Well then, let's jump right in. What exactly happened?

Alfred: My friends and I were having lunch. I saw that my friend had potato chips with ridges. My mom gave me pretzels, which I don't like anywhere near as much. My friend traded me—one for one—and we exchanged a total of twelve. I got the better end. I was quite happy.

Coach: Does your friend like pretzels, or was he just being nice?

Alfred: He said he liked pretzels well enough, and also, he mentioned needing my help on a math problem at the end of lunch. So, it all worked out. I got chips. He got help.

Coach: And do you have one more example to share?

Alfred: Yes. My grandma wanted to get on a Zoom call with me. I hate Zoom. I do love my grandma, but I don't really enjoy talking to her. We only really have my mom in common. Anyway, we zoomed.

Coach: What did you talk about?

Alfred: The worst of all topics—the weather. I guess it is sunny in Florida, where she is right now. I shared that we have snow here in Indianapolis. From there, we discussed her favorite shows. She said she was watching reruns of *Green Acres*, which I never heard of. I told her that I was watching anime on Netflix, which she never heard of. Then we said goodbye. My mom was happy. So was Grandma.

Coach: Wonderful. Ok, I think we're onto our next topic—humor—or as I call it, "Why ha-ha matters." Are you ready?

Alfred: "Def"—that's short for "definitely." I figure you might want to also speak my language. Also "ha-ha" are two one-syllable words. Same with "def."

Coach: Ha-ha. Def. I got it.

Alfred: Well, I can see you're trying. Hey! That means you are wearing my shoes. And since our topic today is humor, I might have just made a joke.

Coach: Do you like to laugh?

Alfred: Of course. Everyone does.

Coach: What types of things are funny to you?

Alfred: Good jokes make me laugh. Sometimes people are funny when they don't mean to be. It would be funny if I were trying to make my mom's Soho Globs. My friends can be funny when they are trying to solve a math problem.

Coach: Before we continue, do you laugh when your friends struggle with a math problem?

Alfred: Never. I think that would be mean. I just laugh inside. I doubt it shows.

Coach: Good. So why do you think we all like to laugh?

Alfred: It makes life more fun. It takes our minds off things that bother us—like will there be friends for me to talk to at lunch? Fortunately, I don't really have to worry about that anymore.

Coach: Alfred, you've identified a lot of reasons that laughter is so important in our day-to-day relationships. I am curious since you said you like jokes, do you have a favorite?

Alfred: Actually, I have a few. What do you get when you cross a vampire with a snowman?

Coach: Something bloody?

Alfred: Not exactly. You get frostbite.

Coach: Clever.

Alfred: Here's another that I like because, as you know, I am very literal. Why did the student eat his homework?

Coach: Why?

Alfred: Because the teacher said it was a piece of cake.

Coach: That joke sounds right up your humor ally.

Alfred: Humor ally? It's not really funny, but I'll give you points for being clever.

Coach: So, there are two ways to engage in humor. One is to be the creator, and the other is to be the appreciator. Not everyone can be a creator. For example, I'm just not funny. However, and there is a "however"—I love to laugh. So, I naturally appreciate that creators give me an opportunity.

Alfred: I like the idea of helping creators. I'm not funny, either. Maybe our laughter helps start a chain reaction or changes the mood.

Coach: Exactly!

Alfred: It's kind of like we're puzzle pieces, fitting together. Someone makes "a funny," and I laugh, and then others join in.

Coach: You get it. Here's what I want to end with. Friendships are built using a lot of tools. We've discussed some. Curiosity. Parking your smarts so that others can shine. Being generous in ways that don't require money. Wearing someone's shoes. Now, let's add "humor." Humor equals fun.

Alfred: Makes sense. Everyone wants to be around fun people. I bet there is data showing how humor makes for stronger friendships. In my world, we call that a "correlation."

Coach: Alfred, I might have to have to work hard to keep up with you.

Alfred: Now that's funny. You just became a creator. I'm back to trying to keep up with you.

Coach: This week's homework will be to experience and report back on two moments of humor. I don't care if you were the creator or appreciator.

Alfred: Got it. Question though. If I decide to literally put on a friend's shoes as kind of a joke, can it be both literal and figurative? If I stumble in them, it might be funny. If I learn something, it might fill the original purpose. You ok with that?

Coach: Yes, and I like that it sounds genuine. You need to be you. Before we call it a day, I need to share with you my reaction to what you wrote regarding the lunchroom. I've been coaching people for a long time, but I don't remember feeling as happy as I did when I read your essay. You are a quick study, and you show guts. You are willing to put yourself out there. You used the word "splendor"—well, maybe it was your mom's word—but nevertheless, I think that is exactly what your words revealed. You are showing all your splendor. Best of all, you wrote this without my asking. Thank you.

Alfred: And I am guessing that what we just showed was generosity in action. I explained my world without you asking, and what I wrote made you happy. Then you said nice things which made me happy.

Coach: You got it. Is this a good time to use "def?"

Alfred: Sure, and I like that you are trying. Just like me.

Coach gives Alfred's mom the update. "Today, we discussed the role of humor in establishing friendships."

Alfred's mom is puzzled. "Alfred and I—we aren't very funny people. How's that going to work?"

"Well, you know that there are creators and appreciators, and both are needed," explains Coach.

"Ok, but can I add a small something?" asks Alfred's mom.

"Sure, especially if it's funny."

"It's not. I know that Alfred and I are both unusual. Maybe you could teach us how to laugh at ourselves."

"Eleanor, that's a great idea, but we will need to work our way up to that. Are you and Alfred patient people?"

At the thought of being patient, Alfred's mom breaks into laughter. "Now that's funny."

"All right, then. I'll catch you next week," Coach says. As he leaves, he is talking to himself and emitting a small chuckle.

"We've got the apples, and we've got the tree. Boy, are they close."

Chunk 7:

A Review Before Winter Break

*C*oach is pretty sure that Alfred is ready for a break. Even still, he wants to make sure that they finish the year out strong.

Alfred is starting to think that just maybe they are getting close to the finish line, even though the meetings have been better than he expected. He did say that they would need no more than one-digit's worth, so at most, that would leave only two more sessions. Best of all, Alfred has started gaining friends, so how much more is really needed?

With no "lesson" in mind other than to review last week's topic of humor, Coach wants to explore what Alfred has found helpful and what he might like next. In the back of his mind, Coach reminds himself that "Easy does it."

Coach: Alfred, good to see you. This will be our last time meeting for this calendar year. How do you feel about that?

Alfred: Good. My time with you is better than I expected, but I'm ready for a break.

Coach: You know, two opposite feelings can exist simultaneously and still be true. We call that "tension." You've been good with our sessions, and you're happy not to have one next week.

Alfred: Yep, that sums it up. But I would say it differently. On a scale of one to ten, I rate you an eight for being helpful. You know tens are impossible, and nine is exceptional, and you fall a little below that. On that same scale, though, my need for a break is a perfect ten.

Coach: Score! I'm good with an eight. Before we get into the topic of humor—which is where we left off last week—you started today exactly where I wanted to go, which is on the topic of feedback. You just shared your thoughts which I really appreciate. How would you like my feedback on our time together?

Alfred: I'd like it. You often say smart things.

Coach: That is a real compliment coming from you. So here it goes. Alfred, you have done a great job taking what I say and putting it to use. You have figured out that your smarts can be a gift to help others, and you do it in a nice way. You show humility. And I am very glad that your lunchroom experience is different now.

Alfred: Yes, I am happy about that too.

Coach: Also, you are working hard to see the world through others' eyes—like when you are trying to figure out what your friends don't see in solving a math problem. But for me, what I am most struck by is your age. You often sound like an adult—not someone who just turned fourteen. Maybe it's due to your intelligence or that you've spent so much time with your mom. But you just sound older and more mature to me.

Alfred: Thank you. I often feel older than my friends—and you should notice that I said "friends" which is plural. I haven't counted, but I'd say more than a handful.

Coach: So now that we've shared some feedback, your "perfect eight" of a Coach wants to go back to humor which is where we left off. Can you share two funny moments from last week?

Alfred: Sure. There is a boy named George who is tall, athletic, and always wears red Converse hightops. I finally did the act of "wearing someone's shoes." I asked George if I could wear his hightops during recess.

Coach: That's kind of bold.

Alfred: Yes, it was. I thought of my favorite anime character—Naruto. He's a young ninja warrior who dreams of becoming a leader. So, I pretended I was Naruto and asked my question, and George said, "Ok." Just like that.

Coach: Then, what happened?

Alfred: Well, George's shoes were big on me, but I still got to run around in them—only I didn't run like him. He's fast.

The hightops themselves are tight around the ankle and super uncomfortable. I thought to myself, "George is kind of like his hightops—tight." He doesn't say much, and he keeps to himself. Coach is right.

Coach: I don't recall offering an opinion on George. (*silence*) Oh, I get it. You understood something about George when you wore his shoes. Well, what was the funny part?

Alfred: There were two, actually. When I tried to dribble, and when I tried to shoot. I failed—so badly that we all started laughing.

Coach: Well, at least you could laugh at yourself. Not everyone can. I also like that you experienced exactly what I had hoped. You understood George—literally and figuratively.

Alfred: Yes. I have one more funny story for you. Last Sunday, I made my mom breakfast. She was surprised since I've never done that before.

Coach: What did you make?

Alfred: I poured her Raisin Bran because I know she prefers that over Reese's Puffs, which she finds too sugary. I smelled the milk to make sure it was good. I poured her a glass of OJ. I took one of my Soho Globs and placed it on a napkin for afterward, and best of all, I kept her company while she ate.

Coach: Wow, now that is what I call "a generous spirit." I'm curious, though, where was the humor?

Alfred: Well, we laughed that I "made" her breakfast. I just assembled what we had and put it in a bowl. We discussed what "made" really means, and I ended by saying, "Well, at least I 'made' us laugh." Then we laughed some more.

Coach: Alfred, I'm super impressed. Your story makes me think ahead some. What next? How can I continue to be of help? Answer me this if you will: What have you found most valuable from our time together?

Alfred: Well, it probably wasn't an accident that, out of the blue, I decided to make my mom breakfast.

Coach: Because?

Alfred: Well, my mom was the one who said I needed a coach. I said that I didn't. She said that it would help me make more friends. I said I was fine. She said that I was better than fine as a person but that I could be happier—that friends were great and that she knew so because she wished she had more of them.

Coach: Wow, I didn't know all this.

Alfred: It's not something you like to share. It's kind of personal. Anyway, she was right. Friends are helpful. My lunches are better. I learned that my mom was right.

Coach: And did our time together help you build friendships?

Alfred: Well, as I like to say, "We're trending in the right direction." That's the numbers guy in me. I eat lunch with my classmates. I help them with their math. I know people's names without writing them on my hands. And they call me by my name, which turns out to be my favorite word. Oh, and I've made my mom happy.

Coach: So, what's next?

Alfred: Well, first, I need a break. I need to watch my shows and not think or do anything while I eat some globs. But don't worry. Come January, I'll be ready—though our sessions won't be a forever thing—just so you know. I said "one digit" which would leave us two more. Maybe there will be some more after that, but we'll see.

Coach: I know we're not forever, but as long as I have you, I want to make sure that I help you with any specific needs or questions that you might have. I think of what we're doing as taking on personal challenges in "chunks". So, if you have chunks that you can identify as needing some attention, please give me my homework.

Alfred: Now, that is kind of funny—me giving you homework. But I don't want to think right now. I want to just be happy that we've done something good. I mean, I "made" my mom breakfast. And now she knows, and I know that she was right when she sent me to you.

Coach: Ok, we'll leave it there. Thank you for being open with me. That's not always easy—for kids or grown-ups, or even kids that seem like grown-ups.

Coach checks in Alfred's mom before leaving. "So, I heard that Alfred made you breakfast the other day," Coach says.

"Yes, what a surprise," responds Alfred's mom. Then, as almost an afterthought, she adds, "The best part was when he told me that I was right about friends being important."

After some silence, Coach offers, "Well, I'll see you in January. We can pick up where we left off."

"One more thing, Coach. Alfred has shared with me the difference between understanding things literally versus figuratively. I find that useful because I run on the literal side. Like, I know we have more work on *our plate* for next year, and at the same time, I want to thank you, so I made you *a plate* of Soho Globs. Get it? Both figurative and literal at work."

Coach is grinning as Alfred's mom continues. "The thing is that Alfred and I aren't very good with words or showing our emotions, but I think my globs say it all. You're actually coaching me too."

With a wink of his eye, Coach says, "I will probably never enjoy eating my words as much as when I eat your globs, Eleanor. Thank you. Happy holidays."

Chunk 8:

Can a Backtrack Be a ZigZag?

After winter break, Coach and Alfred are back at the helm. It's their first time together in three weeks, and Coach is wondering where they should pick up. But then he reminds himself, "Alfred will definitely have something to say. I'll follow his lead."

Coach thinks of the phrase "calling an audible" and wonders whether Alfred's love of sports extends to football. Coach decides he is going to test his range and see what they both learn.

Coach: Hey, Alfred! It's so good to see you. I don't know about you, but I missed not seeing you for three whole weeks.

Alfred: Well, it wasn't quite three whole weeks, but it was close. I actually enjoyed the time by myself. No thinking, no trying to learn something new. Just watching Naruto, eating Soho Globs, talking with my mom some. I am glad you missed me, though. That makes me happy.

Coach: *(chuckling)* Well, you're easy to get used to. I enjoy that you're unique—an "original," as they say. So, tell me, how does it feel to be back in school?

Alfred: I'd like to say "great" but the truth is that it's kind of weird. My mom says that I just need to get back into the rhythm, but that is the kind of thing she would say that really doesn't help me at all. Maybe you'll have something better to offer me.

Coach: I seem to recall that you went into the break feeling pretty good.

Alfred: Yes, but that was almost three weeks ago. It's been hard to pick up where I left off.

Coach: And when you say, "It's hard," what do you mean?

Alfred: I mean that the conversations aren't easy. I think the progress I made might be lost.

Coach: It just feels that way, but you really haven't lost anything. Many people feel awkward when they return to school. And besides, our "normal" path is really a zigzag. We only sometimes go straight. Do you know the expression, "Two steps forward, one step back?"

Alfred: Not really, but I got the "one-step-back" part down. I like the "zigzag" idea, though. I could actually draw it on my hand if I needed to. Leave it to adults to rename a problem so that it sounds good.

Coach: Well, we all wish for a straight shot, but the truth is that we often don't hold our gains.

Alfred: "Zigzag" is good, but I'm gonna use an analogy that helps explain how I feel. I love baseball. By now, you know that about me. Well, in baseball, when a man is on base, the manager's goal is to keep the line moving. Get more men on. Get more runs scored. Well, I want to keep my line moving—more friends, more laughter, more of everything that is good.

Coach: Great analogy! Just don't get discouraged if the line moves slowly or not at all sometimes. Consider "zigzag" as your new favorite dance step.

Alfred: Even if I don't dance? Also, to say "I'm zigzagging" makes me sound weirder than I am and has no application to baseball, which means I might have a harder time remembering it. Ok. Maybe I'll write "zig" on my hand or draw a zigzag line.

Coach: Just to be clear, you're not weird. You're unique in a great way. Also, I know that you think of yourself as just a numbers guy, but our conversation shows another side to you. You're intuitive. You value communication.

Alfred: (*excited*) I'm not just a numbers guy? Are you sure about that? That feels like maybe a game changer!

Coach: Yes, I could see what a game changer that would be. But the one thing I really know is people—just like you really know baseball—so you'll have to trust me on this. Getting back to your time off, when you and your mom were together over break, what did you do that was fun?

Alfred: Something that wasn't just for my mom? Easy. We played a lot of chess. My mom is a good chess player, and I am getting better.

Coach: What do you like about chess?

Alfred: So many things. You have to be able to see the board and all its possibilities. You need to think ahead. You have to understand your opponent. In my case, that's my mom, so I'm fortunate. I got a bead on her —that's a baseball expression for when outfielders can anticipate where the ball is going.

Coach: Ok, so chess seems like a great source of fun. I've got an idea that you might think is crazy but hear me out. Your only assignment this week will be to consider my idea.

Alfred: Fine, but just so you know, in general, I don't do well with "crazy."

Coach: Let's begin by agreeing that you want school to feel as comfortable as before winter break. Is that accurate?

Alfred: Yes

Coach: So, the next step is to play on something that you love. It's what I call, "Finding a facilitator."

Alfred: The next step? Is that a step forward because, as we discussed, I am moving backward.

Coach: Remember, you're not moving backward—you're zig-zagging. I think you maybe should write "zig" on your hand. Back to my idea, I want you to consider starting a chess club. You can get to know people in a natural way, and the game offers you lots of silence. There will be almost no pressure for conversation.

Alfred: Right off the bat, I have a question. You've taught me that I can't lead with smarts. Does that mean I would have to let them win?

Coach: Great question! Short answer: "no," but it requires an explanation. Let me think about how I can answer this in a way that makes sense.

Alfred: Yes, that would be very helpful.

Coach: Ok, here's what's important. Your friends need to feel that you are trying to help them build their game, even if they lose in the process. You would need to explain things. Caution them. Remind them of a previous game where they made a similar error. Basically, you need to be their coach.

Alfred: Like you?

Coach: Yes, like me. You could win as long as your friends believe you are on their side.

Alfred: Even when I'm not?

Coach: Yes. By "side," I mean that you want to help them get better.

Alfred: I'll think about it but don't get your hopes up. I think this is a good place for us to end today. I need to break in slowly. Hopefully, you don't miss me anymore.

Coach: Nope, we're good. See you next week.

Coach drops in on Alfred's mom for an update. "Alfred and I had a great chat today. He's nervous that he's backtracking, but he's not. He's just re-acclimating."

Alfred's mom looks puzzled. "Backtracking how?"

"Alfred hasn't found the conversations with friends to be as easy as it was, but I explained that life is a zigzag. And then I gave him something to consider," then adding, "I'll let him be the one to share it with you."

Alfred's mom smiles. "I get it. You want Alfred to own the idea."

"Something like that," says Coach.

"Well, they do say 'Ownership is nine-tenths of the law.' See you next week, Coach."

Chunk 9:

Alfred Faces His Fears—Game On!

*A*lfred has given a lot of thought to Coach's idea to start a chess club. On the one hand, it's a natural move that plays to his interests. On the other hand, there won't be any real good chess players to help him build his game.

Ah! Then Alfred remembers that starting a chess club is not about chess as much as it is about building his friendship circle in a way that feels comfortable. When Alfred shared his dilemma with his mom, she gave him absolutely no advice. "You'll figure it out," was all he got.

Alfred decided to talk to his friends about this possible idea. When he did, they were so positive and encouraging that it made him nervous. What exactly were they expecting? And chess is a hard game. "They don't realize that they won't get satisfaction for a long time." Still, he sets those thoughts aside. Coach would have something useful to say.

This was a meeting he was looking forward to. If Coach suggested that starting a chess club might help reduce some of his awkwardness around friends, it would be a small price to pay. "But it would be paying," he says to himself as he enters Coach's office.

Coach: Hello Alfred! Great to see you today!

Alfred: Hey, Coach. We have a lot to talk about, so we better get started. I am glad you're glad to see me, though.

Coach: *(chuckling)* So if we better get started, that means you have something to share. What's on your mind?

Alfred: Well, like you asked, I have seriously considered starting a chess club at school. We don't have one, and it could be a good thing, but I've got lots of questions.

Coach: Shoot.

Alfred: I mentioned the idea of starting a chess club at lunch, and my friends asked me questions that I didn't really have answers to. They wanted to know why the king and queen never change roles. Also, which one is more important?

Coach: Hmm. I would never have thought of that.

Alfred: Me neither. I told them that the roles don't change. Who is more important is harder to answer. You need them both. I mean—if the king goes down, you've lost. But it's hard to win without a queen to lead the way.

Silence. Alfred is thinking…

Alfred: And that wasn't all. They wanted to know if the pawns felt bad that they were so small and had no power.

Coach: And what did you say?

Alfred: I explained that chess pieces don't really "feel" as far as I can tell and that the pawns are actually very important. Besides being strategic in setting up your pieces, they are the only ones that can help you regain a lost queen.

Coach: Did that help?

Alfred: I think so. Some of their questions seemed silly. I think I can say "silly" to you. They wanted to know how we decide who goes first—black or white—and was there an advantage. Then someone said, "Because black lives matter in chess too." He wasn't sure whether he made an important point or was trying to be funny. That left me wondering whether I should chuckle. I am still having a hard time with humor. We may need to come back to that.

Coach: So, how did you leave it?

Alfred: Well, I asked them to think about my idea of a chess club and get back to me. It was fun being able to say that to someone. You always say that to me.

Coach: It's almost as if you are becoming a coach.

Alfred: Well, I wouldn't go that far. But they got back to me right away—the next day—at lunch, actually.

Coach: And?

Alfred: They want to start the club. I think this is good news, but I'm not sure. There were a lot of questions that didn't seem to relate to chess at all, and I know there will be more. Still, they did make me think. I am going to change the chess rule that white pieces always go first.

Coach: And on another note, how was your conversation with your friends? Did it feel less awkward?

Alfred: Well, that is probably the best news. The conversation went so fast that we actually interrupted each other. I know interrupting isn't a good thing, but in this case, I think it was.

Coach: Alfred, I really like what you shared with me. I want to leave you something to think about—an idea I use with adults. I call it "Facing your fears." Sometimes the things we imagine aren't as bad as we thought they'd be. You feared that you lost your conversation skills. Clearly, you haven't. You feared that starting a club might not be a good idea because it would highlight that you are very smart, and you are trying hard to fit in. It seems you are fitting in fine. There will be new fears if you start this club. But you will face them like you did last week. Remember that.

Alfred: Coach, can we have my assignment be that I work on making this club happen? If you want to call it "Facing your fears," I am ok with that. It sounds like it's an expression you really like.

Coach: Yep. That works. I'll go check in with your mom now.

Alfred: Ok. If there is something positive to report, make sure you tell her. She worries too much, and she has no one to share it with. She kinda needs you.

Coach heads over to see Alfred's mom. "Eleanor, I'm here to report that all is good. Alfred had a productive week. He has some ideas brewing, but I'll let him share them."

Alfred's mom chuckles, "Well, he shared that he is considering starting a chess club. Imagine that—my Alfred! I like that he is putting himself out there, but I worry that he'll win every match because he probably will if he tries."

Coach responds, "The amazing thing about Alfred is that everything you worry about, he does too. But he is also trying to grow."

Alfred's mom smiles, "Yes, I like that. To use your kind of language, he is working on his emotional intelligence—EQ, right?"

"Exactly!" responds the coach. "And he has us to support him if he gets into trouble."

As Alfred's mom ushers Coach out, she says, "Thank you, Coach. I'm good with where we are. I remembered in our first conversation, you shared that you "chunk" things into pieces so that nothing will feel too big for Alfred. I think that is what you are doing here, and it is helpful to both of us."

Coach smiles and doesn't quite know what to say. He says nothing.

Alfred's mom fills in the silence easily enough, though. "See you next week. By the way, I'm just curious. Do you play chess?"

Coach smiles. "It depends on your interpretation of 'play.' I'll leave it there."

Chunk 10:

Wanna Join Grand Masters?

*C*hess club is a "go." Alfred is in planning mode. He is surprised at how many details he must manage. There is getting the school's permission, explaining to parents the club, working through the logistics of where it will be, and obtaining multiple chess sets. Alfred wonders whether he will have the patience and ability to teach his friends the game. Otherwise, "What's the point?" he asks himself.

"No matter," Alfred thinks, "I am zigzagging forward, and that feels good. He uses a zig-zag line on his hand to remind him that zagging is where it's at.

Coach: Hello Alfred! So good to see you. How goes it? Do you have something to report about your week of "club-building?"

Alfred: Hey, Coach, and yep, I do. I have a lot to report. The question is, where do I start?

Coach: How about the beginning? That always seems like a safe place.

Alfred: Well, "the beginning" makes the process sound like a straight line. We're mostly traveling in a circle, revisiting the same questions. How big is the club? How often should we meet? Will it be competitive? Can we bring snacks? Do I need to know anything about chess?

Coach: Those seem like answerable questions.

Alfred: For the most part. I don't know how competitive it will be. We can start small, but if it becomes popular, I don't want someone to feel left out by saying, "Sorry, the club is closed." That describes a lot of my life, and we are working hard to correct that.

Coach: Wow, you've learned a lot. And I like that you lead with heart.

Alfred: I don't know what that means but let me go on. The hard part of building this club is getting the details right. We had to find a time that worked, get permission from the school, send a message out, answer parents' questions, and encourage my friends who were nervous but wanted to join. Fortunately, my friend Mitchell helped.

Coach: Mitchell? I haven't heard his name before. Well, maybe I read about him in your piece about the lunchroom. Same Mitchell?

Alfred: Yep, same Mitchell. To be clear, though, you haven't heard many of my friends' names because we haven't been friends for very long. The good thing about Mitchell, other than being a friend, is that he actually knows how to play chess.

Coach: So, did you have your first club meeting?

Alfred: Yes. "Grand Masters" was formed. There are ten of us. Seven have never played chess and don't know a thing—yet. Then there is Mitchell, and Hannah, and me.

Coach: Are you feeling positive?

Alfred: Kind of. I realized the ratio is off. By ratio, I mean the time spent playing quality chess compared to the time spent building this club.

Coach: And so?

Alfred: I've had to ask myself if the ratio being off matters to me.

Coach: Well, does it?

Alfred: I'm not sure. It depends on how we do as a group. If I see my friends learning the game and asking good questions, I'll have fun. I've learned that when I help my friends with math homework, it's a different kind of fun. Teaching chess might be like that.

Coach: Alfred, I'm just curious. Do you have any goals in mind for Grand Masters?

Alfred: Oh, yes! Goals equal direction. I hope I can get us to the point where I can challenge club members and not feel bad about going full force—or almost full force. Right now, I can only really play with Mitchell and Hannah.

Coach: Do you have any particular worries about starting Grand Masters?

Alfred: Well, I know that you are big on "Facing your fears," so here are mine. I worry that I won't be patient enough. I might not have any fun. If so, will I have started something I won't want to continue? And this club takes a lot of people skills, which isn't my strength.

Coach: Alfred, your honesty and self-assessment are great. You never know, though—sometimes a weakness can become a strength. Didn't you tell your friends not to underestimate the value of pawns? Maybe inside you, you have your own personal pawns waiting to cross the board.

Alfred: That is one great analogy. I might even borrow it. Should I credit you if I do?

Coach: No need.

Alfred: I have one last thing to share. Sometimes my mom says that she is getting old before her time. Then I think, maybe it's happening to me. After all, I'm managing people, keeping lots of details in order, having to tell people where to go when, and reminding myself not to finish my friends' sentences. That last one is really hard because I usually know what they are going to say, and it can take them so long to get it out.

Coach: Yes, Alfred, you are maturing, but you are not old before your time.

Alfred: Well, at least I have Mitchell! We can share the work and play some chess on the side. Kind of funny, right? Starting a chess club where we get to play some chess on the side? It goes back to my ratio comment.

Coach: I'll tell you what I like, Alfred. You are breaking down the challenges into pieces—what I call 'chunking it." You've found a pal to share them with, and you are thoughtful the whole way through.

Alfred: Ok, I'll take that. I think I'm done for today. Our conversation has kind of pooped me out.

Coach: Well, we found a good place to stop. Keep working with Mitchell so you can divide and conquer and hopefully have some fun in the process.

Alfred: Roger on that. See you next week.

Coach stops in to talk with Alfred's mom. "We are making progress. Alfred has started the club, and he's having to exercise some new muscles."

Alfred's mom is amused. "Which muscles are those?"

Coach explains, "The kind we call 'people skills.' Listening, encouraging, putting others' needs before yours. For Alfred, that means not much actual chess. Also, the club is presenting lots of little details that Alfred and his friend Mitchell need to manage."

Hearing the name of Alfred's friend elicits a smile from Alfred's Mom. "Well, I am glad to hear we have friends beyond Naruto, and it is always good to exercise new muscles."

"Roger on that," says Coach. "See you next week."

Mom smiles and mutters quietly, "That's funny. Alfred uses that expression."

Chunk 11:

Alfred Struggles with a Math Problem

*A*lfred has only had two chess club meetings, but already he is worried. As he recalls Coach's suggestion to start this club, Alfred muses to himself, "The pleasures of building a chess club have been greatly exaggerated."

Fortunately, Alfred has both Mitchell and Hannah to lighten his load. Both are knowledgeable players, and both will help with the many details that need managing. "I am not going to lie," Alfred tells his partners-in-chess. "This is a lot of work, and I am super thankful that I've got your help."

Alfred is considering whether there is a metric that can be used to track "chess club satisfaction." After all, he measures so many aspects of his life—the time spent watching Naruto, the percentage of math problems he has solved over a specific period of time, the number of times he has worn red in a given week. Alfred doesn't love red.

But regarding chess, Alfred hasn't figured out the metrics. Maybe the number of people issues I have to deal with? Games played? Or even complaints registered? Then there's the tried-and-true measurement using the one to ten scale. In this case, how's the mood of the room? How happy do people seem?

In the meantime, another issue catches Alfred by surprise, and it needs Coach's attention.

Coach: Hey, Alfred! I *(Alfred interrupts mid-sentence)*

Alfred: Coach, sorry to interrupt. You're going to ask me how I'm doing. The answer is fine—well, kind of—but we've got a problem to solve. Can we get started?

Coach: Sure. A problem that you can't solve? I am not used to hearing that from you.

Alfred: Yes, and the strangest part is that it's math related.

Coach: Well, I don't know if I can help with a math problem. You're better than me at math.

Alfred: Oh, you'll be able to help. It's math-related but not actually math. My teacher wants me to jump a grade, and when I said, "No thanks," she said, "Well, at least let's jump you in math."

Coach: Why is that a problem? Jumping a level says that you are excelling. Excelling is great.

Alfred: Great? (*repeats in disbelief*) Great??? I've worked—well, technically *we've* worked—hard to help me build friendships. It's finally happening. Why do I want to change things now?

Coach: That's a great question. The answer might be that you can be more math-challenged without risking much.

Alfred: I'm not sure about the "not risking much" part, but regarding being more challenged, I am very challenged. When I help my friends with their math homework, I have to understand what they don't see. Then I try to explain it to them. Trust me. It isn't easy.

Coach: Ok, but your teacher is saying that by jumping a level, you can grow your own math skills. Plus, you'll probably be surrounded by stronger math students.

Alfred: The last thing I need is more people like me in my world. Just so you know, I consider that a very big and very bad risk. My mom was right when she pushed me to have more friends. I actually was lonely but didn't know it. I think I will explain to my teacher why I want to stay put.

Coach: Just curious, what does your mom say about jumping a level in math?

Alfred: She says it's my decision, which to tell you the truth, I don't like.

Coach: No?

Alfred: No. That means that if I choose wrong, I can only blame myself. Plus, she is older and very smart, so she probably has something useful to say—if she'd just say it.

Coach: I think she has said it. She is saying this is your decision, she trusts you, and only you can decide what's best.

Alfred: But she didn't say that.

Coach: No, but sometimes saying a little is saying a lot. She left it for you to infer.

Alfred: Me—Who doesn't always get people? She wants me to "infer" something? Doesn't the word "infer," mean to read the situation? Isn't that what I am working on?

Coach: Yes, but Alfred, you understand your mom really well.

Alfred: Well, let's get back to my immediate problem. I've asked Mitchell and Hannah what they would do. Mitchell said I should do what I want, which was no help. Hannah said something different.

Coach: What did Hannah say?

Alfred: Hannah said I shouldn't worry about losing my friends if I jump to a higher math class, which by the way, is the ONLY jump I would consider. She said that we would still have lunch and chess club. Also, she said, and here I quote, "Your friendships already have roots."

Coach: And to think that only a few months ago, you didn't even know Hannah. And now you consult her. That's serious progress.

Alfred: And that is why I am stressed. It's a big decision. In the "Facing your fears" category—I know you like that term—I have a new fear.

Coach: The fear being?

Alfred: The fear being that I might give up some friendships in the name of math. I want more people like Hannah, and fewer people like me, in my life.

Coach: But you can have both.

Alfred: So that's a good thought to end on, though I'm not sure I agree. I'll do some more thinking and go back and talk to my mom. Maybe she'll be more helpful.

Coach: More helpful than showing you that she believes you'll figure this out?

Alfred: Yes, more helpful than that. I'm still her son. I think I should be able to get some real advice.

Coach: Ok then. Let's leave it there—no real assignment. You've got a lot to consider. Just saying, though, I'm with your mom on this one. I have faith you'll make a decision that works.

Coach checks in with mom. "Alfred's coming your way, so consider this your heads-up."

"Wow, way to greet me, Coach."

"Well, it's kind of how Alfred greeted me. He is having a hard time deciding whether to jump a level in math. He doesn't want to jeopardize his friendships. He says that you were right to see that he was lonely, and now he is much happier."

"Thanks for the heads-up. I want him to believe that his instincts will serve him well. This means that I will try to be helpful in the most unhelpful way."

Coach looks quizzically as he says, "I knew that you contained your advice for a reason. Just wondering, do you have a preference?"

"Yes. I want Alfred happy. I want him to know that he can figure things out that go beyond math. The word 'range' comes to mind. We're building Alfred's range. Now 'range' will mean something specific to Alfred. He'll think about baseball players that have 'range.' From there, it's a simple jump to becoming what they call a '5-tool-player.'"

"I've never heard that term before, Eleanor. Should I have?"

"Only if you like baseball or have a son named Alfred. Anyway, look it up. We need to help Alfred realize that he has his own tools he can depend on. You will have to help him realize what those tools are."

"Wow, my mind is going a lot of places."

"Coach, there's no way else to say this other than 'You've got a big job.' But Alfred responds to you, so I think the job is not bigger than you."

"Ok, then. I'll be there and I'll get smarter on baseball lingo. Catch you next week."

Chunk 12:

Alfred Learns
He Can Be a 5-Tool Player

*W*hen Alfred's mom suggested that Coach help Alfred build "range," the word got stuck in Coach's mind all week. What specifically was "range," and how did it apply to Alfred? And what would Alfred do when it came time to decide whether to jump a level in math? How big was the risk of backsliding on friendships that Alfred worked hard to build?

It was all this and more that was on Coach's mind. "It's a responsibility that sometimes feels very heavy, but I've been down this path before." He reminds himself of what worked in the past. "I believe in the process, and I believe in the people I help. I believe in Alfred."

Coach realized that in saying these words out loud, he gave himself the pep talk he needed before greeting Alfred.

Coach: Hello Alfred! We've got a lot to discuss today.

Alfred: More than usual? Something besides math? Or chess?

Coach: Well, yes, but first, tell me what you decided about math.

Alfred: *(looking sheepish)* I've decided to jump. Ok, here's some humor for you. It's the only jump I can do—a mental one that's about math.

Coach: I'm proud of you. You thought about it, you asked for some advice, thought about it some more, and then you made your decision. And you even made a joke of it. I like the process. You looked at it from all angles and added some humor.

Alfred: Did you use the word "angles" because we are talking math? Was that a humor comeback to my joke?

Coach: *(laughing)* No, I wasn't that clever. I often use "angles" as another word for "perspective," but I'll gladly take the credit for being funny.

Alfred: You actually weren't funny, but I'll give you credit for trying—even if you didn't try.

Coach: Moving on—I assume the chess club is proceeding well, so can I bring up another topic?

Alfred: Whoa! That's a big assumption. I would say chess is trending in the right direction. My friends show up, learn some moves, eat their snacks, and then want to know when they'll become competitive players. They have no idea how long it will take. I don't want to discourage them, so I simply change the topic. This week we discussed how to best use rooks.

Coach: Sounds wise. I still do have another topic to discuss.

Alfred: Yes?

Coach: Your mom asked me to help you become a 5-tool-player. I have to admit that I didn't know what that meant, but I've done my homework.

Alfred: Wait—she wants me to be a baseball phenom? I can barely throw across the diamond, and I'm slower than a turtle.

Coach: Alfred, she was talking *figuratively*. What does being a 5-tool player mean to you?

Alfred: Simple: Hitting, hitting for power, running, fielding, and throwing.

Coach: That is baseball-specific. But if we take it up a level, can it be about building a range of skills that serve us?

Alfred: Like?

Coach: Well, let's take you. You've got math and chess. You enjoy them, and they help you build friendships.

Alfred: So "5-tools" is an analogy. Now I need to come up with three more. Does appreciating humor count?

Coach: It could, but you've got others. For example, you appear to be a good teacher. I say this because your friends keep on coming back for help with their math, and you're teaching them chess, too. You seem to know how to break down concepts into digestible pieces—chunks so to speak.

Alfred: Like you're doing for me. So now I am at three tools—math, chess, teaching—unless humor counts. I am a strong videogame player. I am aiming to be a good communicator. I will never be a good dancer, but fortunately, we only need five skills.

Coach: You've got the idea. A few skills you've nailed, and a few are under development.

Alfred: I'm curious, though. Why did my mom suggest the idea of a 5-tool-player?

Coach: Because when you were trying to make the decision about whether to jump in math, she wanted you to trust yourself more—to build instincts and judgment. Tools equal confidence, which equals trust in oneself.

Alfred: Ahh…so with tools I could have more faith in my decisions?

Coach: Yes.

Alfred: And it is ok that dancing—which is a very social activity—will never be something I do?

Coach: It's fine. You build a range of skills that feels comfortable. Take me, for example. I am bad at sports but good at listening. I am able to hear what people say and don't say. So that is the start of my range.

Alfred: It's funny that you can hear what people don't say—kind of a contradiction, don't you think? What are you hearing if nothing is being said?

Coach: Alfred, that is your great question for today. You always have at least one. Do you ever say something in your head that you won't let come out? Maybe it would hurt someone's feelings or make you feel awkward.

Alfred: Sure. Hannah made me cookies to celebrate my jumping a level in math. They weren't very good. I really only like Soho Globs. But I thanked her. I didn't say, "Thank you for the cookies. It's the thought, not the taste, that counts."

Coach: I am so glad you didn't say that.

Alfred: Me, too. But then I had to eat one and look like I was enjoying it. I counted to five in my head and quickly gobbled it down. Then I smiled and said, "Delicious," though I didn't mean it. The lie was the right thing to do.

Coach: This sounds like a good place to stop. My assignment for you this week is to give some thought to what five tools you want to be able to claim, even if it's in your future. In other words, you might not possess those skills now. As a bonus option, I'd like you to think about things you don't say but only think in your head. Ask yourself why. Sound good?

Alfred: Grand.

Coach stops in to talk to Alfred's mom. "The 5-tool-player was a great shortcut to explain range."

Mom smiles. "We talk the same language—Alfred and me. It helps me help you help him. That sounds confusing, but you're smart, so I know you get it. Alfred and I are pretty similar, and we are challenged by the same issues."

"Well, I feel very fortunate to have your guidance, and the two of us are helping Alfred help himself. Wow, good to know that I can be equally confusing! Anyway, thank you for your help. Someday, Alfred will thank you too."

As Coach heads out, Alfred's mom hands him a small present. "I figured you might want to know more about Alfred's favorite sport, so here is your very own copy of *Baseball for Dummies*. Enjoy."

Chunk 13:

Alfred Begins to Identify His Five Tools

*A*lfred was amused at the idea that he could be a 5-tool-player if he simply expanded the concept. "It doesn't need to be base-ball-specific," his mom told Alfred when they discussed it over dinner one night. "I think Coach called it 'an a-na-lo-gy,'" emphasizing each syllable to make her point.

The idea of five tools not being literal and specific to baseball was so freeing to Alfred that he decided to write something to get himself started. "This is important work," Alfred thought. "It could be the start to a whole new beginning." And so, he wrote something for himself that he would then give to Coach. He didn't know if what he wrote was good, bad, or somewhere in between, but then he reminded himself that this was an instance where he wasn't being graded. "Wow, freedom feels so good," as he finished writing his short piece.

Coach: Hey Alfred. How's it going?

Alfred: I'm good—and loaded with answers and questions for you.

Coach: Great. Let's start with the answers.

Alfred: Ok. You wanted me to identify my five tools, some of which I have and others that I need to work on.

Coach: Right. If you had them already mastered, you wouldn't need me.

Alfred: Well, not exactly. And actually, I never thought I needed you. Only now I realize that I kinda do. Anyway, I wrote something that I will leave you with, but I can tell you where I landed. Let's start with the obvious. Math and chess. Then comes the one you suggested—teaching. I like that because I am, in fact, doing that.

Coach: So that leaves us two more.

Alfred: Yes, I know. I'd like to add baking—specifically Soho Globs. I bet you didn't see that coming.

Coach: Right again. Why'd you pick Soho Globs as a tool?

Alfred: Well, they make me happy. I can bake them for others and make them happy. It's an easy way for me to be generous. And it shouldn't take me long to learn, unlike my last tool.

Coach: Now you've got me curious. What's the last tool?

Alfred: This one will surprise you the most. Just like Soho Globs, it's about people. I want to learn how you hear what's not being said. As you know, I am very literal. It's only the words that people say that I hear. But now I know that there are words that aren't said, and they also matter. So, I want to figure out how to hear them—you know, the words in our head.

Coach: Wow (*silence*). Alfred, you have me speechless.

Alfred: Is that a joke or a strategy? Am I supposed to hear what you are speechless about?

Coach: (*laughing*) No, not at all. I am impressed with your last goal, and I am trying to figure out how to explain it.

Alfred: Start by telling me how you even know that there are words people are thinking but not saying. Then you can explain how you figure out what those words are.

Coach: Ok, but first, a word of caution. You know how you said that your friends want to be competitive chess players, and it will take some time. The same applies here. I am going to give you some tips, but it will take time.

Alfred: Got it.

Coach: Ok. I think what I do—I need to think about what has become instinctive— is ask myself whether what someone is presenting to me makes sense. If there is some logic missing, or a step that didn't happen that should have, I get watchful.

Alfred: I need an example.

Coach: Of course. Let's say you and your friend Mitchell have a big disagreement. You're co-managing the chess club, and he decides to have a tournament, only he didn't tell you until after the details were complete. How would you feel?

Alfred: Angry. Left out.

Coach: When you share this hypothetical story with me, you end by saying, "No big deal." I'd wonder why.

Alfred: So would I. It makes no sense—especially my response.

Coach: I'd start to wonder what aren't you saying? Are you saying that you don't care about chess? That you hate conflict with friends? That you wished you had been the one to think of Mitchell's idea?

Alfred: So, your point is that you saw something in my reaction that made you think.

Coach: Yes. Then comes visual cues. I'd look to see whether you are making eye contact or looking down when you speak. Are your words full of starts and stops, or are you talking with confidence and fluidity?

Alfred: What if the person you are looking at only speaks in starts and stops?

Coach: Then you go to the final step. Ask yourself how you would feel.

Alfred: So those are the three steps? Apply logic? Examine how the person is speaking? And ask yourself how you would feel in their shoes?

Coach: Pretty much.

Alfred: It's funny that it always comes back to being in someone's shoes. I thought we were done with that lesson.

Coach: We're never done with that one. Especially when you want to hear words that aren't said.

Alfred: One more question. Would I be allowed to give someone Soho Globs that I baked in exchange for their sharing the words in their head? Is that a bribe or just being thoughtful?

Coach: It's only a bribe if that's how you think of it. It might just be an act of kindness.

Alfred: Hmm. This week I am going to ask my mom for a baking lesson which will surprise the heck out of her. Maybe I can try to read her thoughts when I ask.

Coach: Good for you—you've identified the assignment that I was going to give you.

Alfred: I can tell by your smile that you like it. And you didn't say a word. And speaking of word, or words, I wrote something that I am going to leave you with. You got me thinking last week, and I felt a need to write something.

Coach: Thank you, Alfred. I especially like that on your own volition, you chose to write something. I look forward to reading it.

Coach stopped by to check in with Alfred's mom. "You'll never guess where we landed today."

"I probably won't, but I hope it's related to being a 5-tool player."

"Yes, it is. I'll let Alfred share one of the tools where you have a small cameo. Another tool, though, is highly aspirational. He wants to learn how to read people better. Specifically, he wants to hear what people think but don't say."

The room was momentarily filled with silence while Alfred's mom just looked at Coach. Coach simply could not tell what this unspoken moment meant, but he knew it meant something. First, he saw a smile form, and then a tear ran down her face. He still chose not to fill the silence but to wait.

Finally, Alfred's mom offered, "You can probably tell that I feel moved right now. I won't ask how Alfred landed on hearing the unspoken, but it is something I struggle with—a lot. Maybe I will ask Alfred whether he can be my teacher after he learns."

"Eleanor, Alfred would probably really like that. I'm here too."

"Thank you, Coach—once again."

Chunk 14:

Note to Self:
Me as a 5-Tool-Player

*W*ho knew I could be one?

It feels odd to write something when I don't have to. I mean, if I were going to do something voluntarily that felt like homework, it would probably be to solve a math problem—90% likely that's what I'd pick. But instead, here I am writing about my five tools. I like Coach's suggestion, though, because it's as close as I will get to feeling like a baseball player. After all, I can't run fast, or throw across the diamond, or even swing a bat and make clean contact. There will never be a "go yard" moment for me—other than watching a homerun on television.

But picking five tools that aren't about baseball might just be how I go yard. My mom uses a different word. She uses the word "mature." "Alfred," she'll say, "I know that sometimes you feel awkward and maybe even lonely, but I also know that you are going to mature. You will become well-rounded, and your world will be just fine."

My mom has some of it right. I do sometimes feel awkward, though less so today as I write this. I don't think I'm lonely, but maybe she knows something that I don't. And I'm not sure what "well-rounded" really means. I hope it doesn't mean "rounded belly." No, I think she means that there will be new things that I bring to me and to the people in my life. "People" is a funny word because it's really more like "person," which is my mom. Unless we count Coach and Grandma, though, I do have some friends in the making. Ok, I'll count Hannah and Mitchell.

Anyway, between Coach asking me to consider my five tools and my mom suggesting that I will "mature" just fine, I decided to write down my list. Just having a list already makes me feel more mature. I'll share them with Coach and maybe at some point with my mom. So here are the five tools that I want to develop.

#1: Math: There is simply not enough math in our world. Also, there aren't enough people who appreciate math or feel comfortable solving math problems. This is where I imagine myself wearing a superman cape plastered with geometry symbols and coming to the rescue of all mankind. But for now, we'll start with helping my friends.

#2 Chess: This is something I am getting better at with each passing night. "Night" because that is when I play chess with my mom, which happens before we watch *Friends*. In some ways, chess is like math, but I think there is maybe more strategy involved, and you are playing against someone. In math, I am only playing against the problem. Coach thinks chess might be a way for me to build more friendship skills. You concentrate on playing and only talk a little.

If I can have fun doing something I like and make more friends, then that is a win — no matter whether I've won the game or not.

#3 Teaching: Proof that I can do this relates to #1 and #2. I am always helping my friends with math homework. It is harder to help them than to simply solve the problem myself, but that's where teaching comes in. I need to understand what they don't see and then explain it. I think I am starting to do this. The same thing in chess. So it might be that I don't have the skills today to call myself a "teacher," but I think I am building them, and those skills are helping me make friends.

Yes, it all comes down to the ways that I can "expand my circle." That phrase is my mom's, but I like it because circles take me back to geometry.

#4. Soho Globs: This sounds like a gimme but making a good glob will probably not be easy. Why I want this as a skill is because of what I call a "twofer." Two good things result. I can have a continuous supply of globs that doesn't depend on my mom's schedule, and I can use them as a way of showing generosity. I mean, who wouldn't appreciate a rich, dense but still soft chocolate cookie?

I know from Coach how important generosity is in building friendships — probably in keeping them too. This would be my way of showing generosity. Maybe I'll call it my "signature move." That's an expression sport announcers use sometimes when they describe a player's unique skill. I would happily claim this as mine.

#5. Hear the unspoken: This is a weird one that I wouldn't have identified or understood until a week ago when Coach and I talked about how important it is to hear what people think but don't say. Coach also explained how we do this using some logic. It's three simple steps: Consider whether what the person is saying makes any sense. Then look at the person and see if they are making eye contact. Eye contact strongly correlates with truth-telling. Finally, I should consider how I would feel if I were in their shoes.

When I shared tool #5 with my mom—because I figure she might benefit too—she said, "So it has to pass the smell test." That made no sense to me since we weren't smelling anything, but then she explained it was a figure of speech. I am very literal, so then I understood my confusion. I am still not sure I understood the expression.

There isn't room for a sixth tool because I am limited to five, but if I did have a sixth, it would be to know which questions to ask and maybe how to gently ask them. There is a lot that I wonder about, but don't ask. There are questions I'd like to ask my mom, but I worry they would upset her. Maybe if she hears the unspoken, using the logic that I just shared, she will come to see I've got some questions that need answers. We'll save that for another time.

I am going to end this note to myself by referencing one of my all-time favorite characters in literature. I love Gandalf, the wizard in *Lord of the Rings*. He is wise, great with people, and a believer that things will work out. He brings hope to the world, and he solves problems all the time. He leads in the nicest of ways.

Now I want to address Coach:

Coach, if these tools can in any way help me to be like Gandalf (and yes, I know he is fictional but still), I will be proof that, as you say, "Tools equal confidence." And you added, "With confidence, I can trust myself more." That sounds very good and also where I want to be.

I am now committed to working on these five tools. It is a full list, but with a little help from you and my mom, I think I can get there.

Chunk 15:

Hearing the Unspoken

Coach was moved by Alfred's taking the time to commit to writing what his five tools might become. With every passing encounter, Coach would reconsider Alfred's age. "He brings so much to our conversation—maturity and depth. I wonder if spending so much time with his mom enabled this," he thought.

There were other ways in which Alfred seemed younger and more innocent than his peers. He hadn't been part of any group and, as a result, hadn't learned some of the more challenging behaviors from his peers. This combination of maturity and innocence made Alfred a kind of walking contradiction.

Coach had also begun to wonder whether they were approaching the point that he should "set the fledgling free." Coach liked that expression because it spoke to the core of what he was trying to accomplish. Coach wanted to be the invisible hand helping his clients until no help was needed. The moment of extrication was a judgment call, but Coach felt confident he would know when his time with Alfred was up.

As Coach prepares to meet Alfred, he considers Alfred's interest in hearing the unspoken word. This feels to Coach like a good place to start, even if Alfred throws something unexpected his way, which he often does.

Coach: Wow! What's this? Do I see Soho Globs?

Alfred: Yes, you do. Made by me. That's the special part. That smile on your face tells me all I need to know. Don't say a thing.

Coach: I see you are rapidly progressing in hearing the unspoken.

Alfred: Well, I wouldn't say that. I would say that you're a slam-dunk. My mom is much harder. I couldn't tell whether she was happy or annoyed when I asked her to teach me how to make Soho Globs.

Coach: What did she say?

Alfred: Just to remind you, we are working on what my mom didn't say. What she said was, "ok." We say "ok" to each other all the time. But what was she thinking? Maybe, "Why does Alfred want to learn this? Do I even have the time? Will he clean up afterward?" It often comes back to cleaning up.

Coach: And you didn't ask her what she was thinking?

Alfred: No. Isn't that what I'm working on figuring out?

Coach: Yes. As you wrote and I read, it's the fifth skill you intend to bring to your world. I think you are well on your way. But back to your mom, when you figure out exactly what she was thinking, please let me know. That would be proof positive that you've got the skill.

Alfred: When I know, you'll know, but I've got another problem to share.

Coach: Shoot.

Alfred: My friends and I were in chess club the other day. They were repeating the same stupid mistakes that they'd made before. They leave their queen too exposed. I've told them this. They haven't learned.

Coach: And so?

Alfred: Well, two things happened. I got irritated, and I didn't use my words well. I said, "You've done this before, and it didn't end well." Joey, who is probably the slowest one to pick up the game, said: "Well, maybe I'm not as smart as you."

Coach: How did you respond?

Alfred: I said that I was sorry. I also said that my mom says everyone is smart in different ways—which she does say. And I told him I would try again, maybe with a drawing, to show him how he leaves his queen exposed. I know that we all learn in different ways. I plan to add drawings to my list of tools for teaching.

Coach: It sounds like you nailed your response to Joey.

Alfred: Well, not exactly. That is, not if Joey can read the words in my head. I was thinking, "Not this again," and "When will I have fun with this club?" Also, "Do I even want to continue?"

Coach: Those are some very big questions.

Alfred: Yes, they are. You should gobble a glob—I say that to my friends, and they laugh. It almost makes me funny. Anyway, globs help you think. At least, they help me.

Coach: Ok but back to your questions while I gobble a glob.

Alfred: Yep—so why my outburst? I think I hurt Joey's feelings. I also think the problem is that I went from no people in my life—other than my mom—to so many people. So much talking. So much listening. So much answering questions. So much being polite.

Coach: Yes, but our goal was more people in your life. Right?

Alfred: Yes, but now I am tired. I need a break.

Coach: And you're wondering if you can give yourself a break and not undo your progress.

Alfred: As my friends say when someone is right, "Ding, ding, ding."

Coach: Alfred, you never fail to surprise me. For a guy who loves math, and numbers, and statistics, and chess, you are as sensitive and people-centered as they come. You have just identified a limit for yourself.

Alfred: Thank you, I think—by the way, 'thank you' is not over-used. I've noted that you and I often overuse "ok" too—just so you know. Anyway, when I am at school, I sometimes can't wait to go home, play video games, and hang out with Naruto, who isn't even real.

Coach: Not to worry. We can handle your needing some down-time. This challenge is not bigger than us.

Alfred: Because?

Coach: Because until now, we hadn't gotten to the point where we needed to tone things down. Now we have. You need a break. That's what your instincts are telling you. We all need breaks. We also need instincts to guide us.

Alfred: Instincts could be on my list of tools to work on, but my list is full. I'm not convinced I have 'em. So, what's my assignment?

Coach: You have no assignment other than to relax and re-charge. Eat cookies, play video games, and keep up with your schoolwork. Tell Mitchell and Hannah that they're in charge of the chess club this week.

Alfred: Really? That's ok?

Coach: More than ok. It's great. Ok? See you next week.

Coach dutifully stops by to check in with Alfred's mom. "I just had a very interesting chat with Alfred."

"How so? Did he tell you we made Soho Globs?"

"He more than told me. He gave me some and then told me to gobble one up because 'It helps one to think.'"

"Anything major I should know about?"

"Well, it finally dawned on Alfred that while he needs people, he also needs alone time. And this need kind of frightened him."

Alfred's mom says pensively, "I wondered when that would happen—when he might feel suffocated by all the activity and new friends. It occurred to me when we were making Soho Globs."

"Really?"

"Yes, and I was thinking that of the many things you're teaching him, we need to add 'moderation' to the list. That's how Alfred's lessons will stick."

Coach smiles. "Ok, then. I'll add moderation to our growing list. I might be old and gray by the time I'm done."

"Coach, you should know better than anyone—we're never done. See you next week."

Chunk 16:

Refresh, Reset, Timeout

*C*oach is curious about what Alfred had done to refresh, and also, whether one week "off" is sufficient. Coach knows he has been asking a lot of Alfred, but he reminds himself that it's like being an athlete in training. "You need to push yourself to the edge and build some endurance."

In sessions with clients, he has often referenced the need to build "social muscle"—and "that is what dear Alfred is doing" he says to himself. Unspoken words are everywhere.

Coach: Well, I can tell just by looking at you, Alfred, that you are feeling recharged.

Alfred: I know you're good at reading the unspoken, but I'm curious. What told you that in all of three seconds?

Coach: It's the eyes. Your sparkle is back. Also, it's your posture—straight versus slumping.

Alfred: Cool. I need to remember those tips.

Coach: So, tell me about your week.

Alfred: Well, I did as you suggested. I went to school, came home, did my homework, ate my favorite cookies, and watched some Naruto, whose mind is pretty easy to read.

Coach: Sounds splendid. And did Hannah and Mitchell take over chess club for you?

Alfred: Yes—for the week—and I owe them a thank you. That was a good suggestion you had. They were surprised by how hard it is to explain what felt like obvious moves. Mitchell said, "Now it's your turn to run the show." I'm ok with that because, as you say, "I'm refreshed."

Coach: Sounds like a good outcome.

Alfred: Well, mostly. Hannah was irritable. I brought her some globs, but even that didn't help. I told her I really needed to give myself a timeout, and I got no response. Then I asked what was wrong? "Did chess club do this to you?"

Coach: Wow. I like that you went straight to the right questions.

Alfred: Not exactly straight. I thanked her. Then I explained my timeout. Then I gave her globs. And when nothing else worked, I had to ask her what was wrong.

Coach: Did she respond?

Alfred: Kind of, but I don't have the whole answer. That's what you discover when you look for the unspoken. She said something about taking care of her brother. Then it looked like she was about to cry, and she walked away.

Coach: So, what did you do?

Alfred: I went up to her later. I figured she either needed time by herself or was about to cry and didn't want me to see. Later, she was better—at least she seemed so. I told her that if I could help, she should let me know.

Coach: It sounds, then, like you reached out in a quiet kind of way.

Alfred: Coach, you've known me for five months. "Quiet" is my way.

Coach: Yes. When I think of you, "Still waters run deep" comes to mind. But that's for another time. Remind me, though, to tell you why I think that of you, in case I forget.

Alfred: Anyway, the surprise was that later Hannah found me and said she knew a way I could help. I was just hoping it wasn't with her brother because, at this point, I can only take care of myself—and maybe my mom.

Coach: Did she explain how you could help?

Alfred: She said it would take a conversation to be had later. When I asked if it was related to her brother—because I was nervous—she said "no" but that her brother has affected her mood. Her mom is working more hours, and her dad doesn't live near them. I know this from our lunches. And Hannah has had to do more brother-sitting.

Coach: Well, I'll be interested in what she has in mind.

Alfred: Me, too. I can't read this one.

Coach: So back to us—did you learn anything from giving yourself a timeout?

Alfred: Definitely. I didn't know how much I needed my timeout until I had it. I was screaming at Naruto—in a good way—while eating my dinner. My mom let me because she could see I didn't want to talk. Afterward, at school, I enjoyed being with my friends again. They didn't seem to notice that I'd checked out—except for Hannah and Mitchell.

Coach: That's a lot of learning for one week.

Alfred: Yes, it is. I know now that I have to pay attention to my own unspoken words. My mom said that I was just pressing a reset button. I also learned that my friendships aren't so breakable. I came back, and we picked up as if I hadn't disappeared.

Coach: So now we need to think about this week's assignment. I assume you are up for another challenge—now that you've yelled at Naruto and pressed the reset.

Alfred: I'm ready.

Coach: I'd love to see how you engage with Hannah to help her.

You've already started. What is her "ask" of you? Also, I'd like you to think about how you will know in the future that you need a timeout before it hits you—kind of like preventative maintenance. Think of yourself as a car.

Alfred: OK, but just so you know, I much prefer being a 5-tool-player over a car needing maintenance. Anyway, you've given me two excellent assignments. The first one—with Hannah—will be very hard. My mom talks about "tough customers." Hannah might be one. Ok, I gotta go. My world is calling.

Coach checks in with Alfred's mom. "You did a great job in helping Alfred relax. He told me that you even let him eat dinner with Naruto."

"I knew what he needed because I've been there—well, not with Naruto but with not wanting to engage. That was a very important lesson that you led him to."

Coach smiles. "The awesome thing about Alfred is that you just put a few breadcrumbs out there, and he finds the trail. Very little me, very much him."

"So, what's this week's assignment for my refreshed son?"

Coach replies, "Well. It's kind of curious. He needs to help Hannah, who is having a tough time, but he's not sure how."

"Oh, so it's the 'giving back' lesson. Makes sense. By the way, it's not lost on me that we need to give back to you. It might take some time, but we'll figure something out. Next week, then?"

"Yes, and you don't owe me a thing, but I do appreciate your generous spirit. Talk to you next week."

Chunk 17:

An Unexpected Request Stumps Alfred

$\mathcal{J}$ust as Coach is considering how Alfred has fared after resuming his packed schedule, he hears the knock on the door. "Hmm, if that is Alfred, he is five minutes early."

He's certain it's Alfred, and now he's wondering what that means. Is Alfred feeling stressed? Are we now back to where we started?

Only one way to find out …

Alfred: I know that I am early, and if it's a problem, I can wait outside for five minutes, which is the exact amount of time that I'm early.

Coach: Alfred, it's not a problem. Come in.

Alfred: And not to be greedy, but can I start our session this week? I know we begin with the basic greeting first.

Coach: Sure.

Alfred: Great. Hello, and I need some help. Oh, and, I almost forgot, how are you today?

Coach: I'm good. You don't quite have the greeting thing down. Usually, we start with, "How are you?" and then proceed to "I need some help," but that's ok.

Alfred: I hear you, and I appreciate your spoken words. Well, anyway, I finally found out what Hannah wants.

Coach: And?

Alfred: It's something I don't think I can do.

Coach: Alfred, you are the kind of person who can pretty much do anything—you're that good.

Alfred: She wants me to be in a play that she is writing and will direct. She says it's a good way for her to get her feelings out.

Coach: That sounds smart.

Alfred: Yep, but the problem is that I don't act. At least, I don't know how to act. Unless you count the times that I act nice and even patient, but I'm not feeling it. What I am really doing during those moments is talking to myself and saying, "Hang in there. Just a few more minutes of this. Sometimes, I even do a silent count."

Coach: Well, we all act sometimes. In my profession, we have a term for it, which I won't bother sharing now. Basically, we contain our reaction in exchange for social acceptance. It's healthy even if it doesn't feel like it at the time.

Alfred: Ok, but back to me… I told Hannah that I want to help her, but I don't know how to act and am not comfortable doing so. She said not to worry. She'd make me the narrator. I wouldn't have to act — only memorize lines and keep the story going.

Coach: Sounds perfect.

Alfred: How so? I'd still have to be on stage doing something I'm not comfortable with — and only because I want to help Hannah. Why won't baking her some more Soho Globs do it?

Coach: Maybe because she needs more than that? Maybe the globs mean more to you than to her? And just maybe she's scared about what she is taking on, and she needs your support?

Alfred: If only she'd said all that, I would have understood.

Coach: But isn't that why she needs to write? She doesn't yet have words for her feelings.

Alfred: And now you're going to suggest that I put myself in her shoes. Or maybe by saying "yes" to being Hannah's narrator, I am showing a generous spirit.

Coach: Ding, ding, ding. Do I have it right?

Alfred: Yes. You remembered it correctly, but you don't sound as good saying it as when my friends do. Anyway, if this is about Hannah trying to understand her feelings, why can't I suggest that she talk to you?

Coach: Mostly because that is not where she seeks her comfort right now. Also, whether it's talking to a coach or writing a play, it still comes back to Hannah using her words.

Alfred: Or me using her words if I become her narrator.

Coach: How about you see this as a growth opportunity? Maybe you will get to learn something new about yourself.

Alfred: Like?

Coach: Like what it is to be center stage.

Alfred: That's exactly what I don't want!

Coach: Ok, how about this. Let's reframe this as an opportunity to create something collectively with friends.

Alfred: Coach, back when we discussed humor, didn't we decide that I was more of an appreciator than a creator?

Coach: Well, we are far more than our labels, and anyway, that conversation was specifically about humor. Just to point out, you create all the time. You created a chess club. You are creating new friendship skills. Showing up as Hannah's narrator could mean a lot.

Alfred: I'll think about it. Can we change topics for the last few minutes? I'd like to use the five minutes we have left for something else.

Coach: Sure, but before we do that, I need to give you one of my favorite quotes. It comes to mind because you very carefully measure our minutes. There is a famous poet named T.S. Eliot, and in one of his poems, he has a line that goes, "I have measured out my life with coffee spoons." You might be doing that regarding these five minutes. And just so you know, that line is deep and not really about coffee at all. Now back to the topic you want to discuss. What is it?

Alfred: Ok, and by the way, I don't like coffee so I am unlikely to use that line. Anyway, I am enjoying chess club more, so that's good. I am getting used to the new math class, which is definitely harder, and I think that's good. I don't have friends in the class, and I'm not sure that I want to have friends in that class.

Coach: Ok.

Alfred: And I will probably tell Hannah that I will be her narrator, even though I still wish she could just talk to you and get her words out that way.

Coach: You know the expression, "To each their own?"

Alfred: No, and anyway, you've just given me "coffee spoons" to think about. How many non-numerical expressions can I hold in my head? Anyway, let's begin with what I know. I have a lot going on, and I can't just give myself timeouts all the time. Especially if I have to be rehearsing—which I haven't decided is a definite.

Coach: So, what's your question?

Alfred: I'm not sure there is a question. I am feeling tired, and it hasn't even begun. I think my question is, "What's a good way to stay calm?" I want to believe I can do all this and stay happy.

Coach: Great question! I can always count on you for at least one question that almost stumps me.

Alfred: I'm not trying to stump you. If I wanted to do that, I'd give you a math problem. *(Alfred smiles)*

Coach: And that would probably do it. Ok, I want you to think about an expression I used last week: "Still waters run deep."

Alfred: What do I do with that?

Coach: Your assignment is to tell me what that expression means and why it makes me think of you.

Alfred: Ok, but can "still waters" replace "coffee spoons?" I like water way more, so there is a better chance I will understand it. Also, I really hope there is an answer buried in those words. I need an answer.

Coach: There will be.

Alfred: I am going to trust you on this. Math is so much easier. It makes so much more sense. I'll see what I can come up with, but just so you know, I am not feeling very "still" inside.

Coach checks in with Alfred's mom. "Does the expression, 'Still waters run deep' mean anything to you?"

"Yes, but why are you asking?"

"Because Alfred is stressed, and I gave him that expression to think about. He wants to help Hannah but not in the way she wants. I won't say more. But besides being a 5-tool player, I want Alfred to see his depth."

"And by sharing that with me, you are maybe hinting that I can be of help to my son?"

"Pretty much," smiles Coach. "You are smart and intuitive, which is where Alfred gets it. And you know how to take the seeds that I plant and throw some water on them. Does that work for you?"

"Yes, it does, and I like where you're going. Catch you next week."

Chunk 18:

Getting to "Yes"

*C*oach suspects Alfred is feeling more comfortable because he hasn't arrived early, as happened last week. Coach is curious whether Alfred finally committed to being in Hannah's play and also whether Alfred could find any meaning in the expression "Still waters run deep." Coach puts the odds at greater than fifty percent. Then he wonders, "I haven't done that before—given something odds. Is Alfred having an effect on me?"

For Coach, measuring life in coffee spoons is an apt image, but he reminds himself, "I am an adult, and Alfred—no matter how old he seems—is a young teen." While he muses on all this, he hears the knock.

Coach: Hey Alfred! Good to see you. I assume it's my turn to start today's greeting.

Alfred: Ok, but I'll give you a heads-up. I'm still going to skip asking how you are and get straight to how I am—which is nervous.

Coach: Why? Are you still debating whether to join Hannah's cast?

Alfred: No—I'm done debating. I said yes. I hope I don't regret it.

Coach: I think you chose right. In case you're worried about appearing foolish on stage, you won't. You don't have foolish in you. Anyway, most of the things we worry about never come to pass.

Alfred: Well, if we are done with the greetings, I'll tell you why I said yes. It was two things I heard in my head—one from you and one from my mom. You told me to have a generous spirit. Saying "yes" is definitely generous. And my mom frequently tells me to keep an open mind. That's what she said that when I told her I didn't need a coach. "Alfred, keep an open mind. It's going to help you in life."

Coach: Your mom is right about keeping an open mind. So, what was Hannah's reaction? I assume you told her.

Alfred: She thanked me—and then asked if she needed to make me Soho Globs to show her appreciation. I told her no because no one makes them better than my mom, and anyway, it was my turn to be generous. If she made them, it would only be my turn again.

Coach: You got a point.

Alfred: Then Hannah told me the name of the play, and I had to keep my thoughts to myself—you know—unspoken words. I also had to remember my mom's words to keep an open mind.

Coach: What is the play's name?

Alfred: I'll tell you, but don't laugh. I almost did. *"Popposites—the Pop of Opposites."*

Coach: I like it.

Alfred: You do?

Coach: Yes. It suggests complexity. And the word "pop" sounds hopeful and fun.

Alfred: Hannah gave me some examples like the strict teacher who actually is very kind. Also, when you cry and laugh at the same time, you have popposites. Her grandma died, which was very sad, but she was a funny lady, so they laughed at things she had said—while they were crying. Even me being on stage might be a popposite. I don't act, and yet I will be their narrator.

Coach: Oh, the places you can go with popposites.

Alfred: Also, Joey is part of the cast. He is better at stage than at chess. It turns out that Joey is good at building things. Remember when I hurt his feelings because he repeated the same stupid mistake in chess, and then I apologized and told him that people are smart in different ways? Well, this week, I found out one of the ways that Joey really is smart.

Coach: So, it's not just about the play. You are proving yourself to be open-minded about how you see people. That's even more important. It's like a math problem where you are introducing new data before drawing a conclusion.

Alfred: You sort of make me nervous when you compare things to math. Maybe we can just say that having an open mind is another tool. Then I could be a 6-tool player. That's better than Mike Trout, my favorite 5-tool baseball player.

Coach: You started today by telling me that you're nervous. I am guessing that chess, drama, and school still feel like a lot.

Alfred: And don't forget about reading unspoken words. It's exhausting. I thought about your saying, "Still waters run deep," but it didn't help. I need some spoken words here, please.

Coach: The saying is a little like "*Popposites.*" We are deeper and more capable than what appears on the surface. Let's take you— very smart, excellent at math, a competitive chess player. And now you've discovered what friends add to your life. And you are about to go even deeper and be a better friend to Hannah. So, don't be fooled by your surface.

Alfred: Ok. But what do I do with this?

Coach: You remind yourself that going deep is half the fun— that you are more capable than you thought.

Alfred: Can you turn this saying into an assignment for me, but one that doesn't take too much time? I'm kind of busy, but this sounds important.

Coach: Sure. Make a list of the things you will need to do for a successful stage debut. For example, you'll need to memorize lines. Of course, there's more. Let's look at the list next week and see which will be laydowns and which will stretch you. We will aim to replace fear with fun, shallow with deep. Oh—and don't forget to give yourself a timeout. That's super important.

Coach checks in with Alfred's mom. "I would say we're in a bit of turmoil as Alfred leaves his comfort zone. Keep an eye on his stress level, maybe?"

"Will do. Soho Globs and Naruto should provide some good couch potato time. I'm curious, though. Did you explore Alfred's still waters'?"

Coach smiles. "Yes, and we're working through how he keeps an open mind in exploring his depth."

"Scary stuff—for Alfred and for me. And when I say 'me,' I mean for me as a mom and me as a person also struggling to understand what's beneath my surface. Oftentimes, I find that the homework you give Alfred is also the homework you give me. Thanks, I think."

"Eleanor, you're welcome, I think. You might want to be careful about what you thank me for. Next week, then."

Chunk 19:

Popposites—Lessons of Another Kind

*L*ast week Alfred and Coach discussed joining Hannah's play *Popposites* as narrator, an act Alfred agreed to solely out of friendship. To change Alfred's view—less fear, more fun—Coach suggested that Alfred draw up a list of skills needed for his new role.

Coach: Hey Alfred! How goes it? I don't want to assume anything, but you look a little tired.

Alfred: Assume all you want. Yes, I'm tired. We started rehearsal, which means more time at school, more kids, more conversation—less downtime.

Coach: Are you enjoying it somewhat? Does it help if you think of it as a learning opportunity?

Alfred: No, and yes. I am not having fun—at least not yet. But I am learning something, and learning is always good. Our teacher, Ms. Baker, is overseeing the play. She makes suggestions, but she also lets Hannah run the show because it is, after all, Hannah's show. Specifically, as you and I know, it's Hannah's words.

Coach: And we respect a person's words, right?

Alfred: Of course. It's another kind of popposite, though. Hannah's words are spoken by someone else, so whose words are they? And can an actor change the words to make them sound more like the actor? And this leaves aside the emotion we give each word which can change the meaning. So, whose words are they, really?

Coach: Great question!

Alfred: I know. *(pause)* It's like when I repeat my mom's words. "Everyone is smart in their own way." My words would be more like, "Do what you're good at. It will make you happiest."

Coach: Just to be clear, though, the meaning of those sentences isn't the same. Your mom is saying to appreciate that there is a wide range of intelligence that we all bring. I think you're suggesting that we should do what makes us happy, which is often what we're best at—except in the case of me singing. I can't hit a note, but it's never stopped me. And the worst part, mostly for others, is that I have so much fun trying, which means that I do more of it.

Alfred: Ok, but can we return to the play and the assignment you gave me?

Coach: Sure.

Alfred: You asked me to make a list of what being a narrator requires. I did. It includes memorizing my lines and learning others' lines so I can help them if needed. I need to pay attention to Hannah and read what she is feeling because I only took this on to be a better friend to her. I won't worry about the acting part since I am just the narrator who keeps the story going.

Coach: Everything you mentioned is well within your range.

Alfred: Yes, but there are challenges. First of all, when people struggle with their lines, and I help them, am I a good friend or a know-betterer? I only want to be a friend.

Coach: I see it as being a friend, but you will have to ask them how they see it.

Alfred: And Ms. Baker could see that the mood was getting tense. People don't know their lines. Joey isn't finished working on the set. Hannah is trying to make sure this isn't a flop, and right now, she can't see how it will be a success. Ms. Baker said, very matter-of-factly, "We need a culture builder here."

Coach: What the heck is that?

Alfred: Exactly. I am so glad you don't know what that means either. She explained that it is someone who pays attention to the mood and lifts the mood when needed. Then, out of the blue, Hannah said, "Ok, Ms. Baker. We'll give that job to Alfred."

Coach: Whoa! To you?

Alfred: Seriously, that was my reaction. I wasn't sure what to even say, and then I heard my mom's words: "In for a penny. In for a pound." All of a sudden, I understood this saying. I guess I'm in for a pound. Sometimes we need to discuss why adults have all these sayings that are supposed to make our world clearer, but not now.

Coach: Ok, Mr. "In for a penny, in for a pound." What will you do as a "culture-builder?"

Alfred: That's what I am trying to figure out. It needs to be my assignment for next week. So far, I have two ideas. Add humor. Help my friends feel successful—like they can nail their role.

Coach: Very thoughtful and creative!

Alfred: As an appreciator, humor is not my strong suit, but I figured that light bulb jokes usually work. Do you know how many librarians it takes to change a light bulb? No, but I know where you can look it up.

Coach: Funny, and it will offend no one.

Alfred: And then there's this one that will feel personal to the cast. Do you know how many skateboarders it takes to screw in a light bulb? Just one, but it takes 20 tries. That's us—take twenty.

Coach: Now you've added wisdom to the humor.

Alfred: Maybe—or maybe just relevance. But I've asked everyone to bring with them a joke tomorrow. Then we can make each other laugh. That's me as "Mr. Culture-Builder."

Coach: You said you had two ideas. What's the other?

Alfred: In the same way you help set me up for success, I might try to help them. But of course, not exactly the same way. More like the same principle. But please don't ask me for the details yet. I don't have them.

Coach: Ok. Well, this seems like a great place to stop. You've got a lot going on. We know the general idea of next week's assignment will focus on you as a culture builder. Do you want to be more specific?

Alfred: Yes. I'm going to figure out how to set up my friends for success. It'll probably be more like a hypothesis. Can I give you a small assignment?

Coach: Sure, but you have me thinking that you really are becoming me.

Alfred: When you hear the assignment, it will remind you that we're different. Figure out who Zeno the mathematician was. Then I can tell you my favorite nerdy joke. See you next week.

Coach checks in with Alfred's mom. "Good stuff today. I am honored to be able to help Alfred help himself."

"Well, it seems like we have some mutual appreciation going on. Alfred feels just as lucky to have you."

Coach continues, "Today, Alfred not only identified his assignment, but he gave me one— if you can believe it."

"No way! What did Alfred assign you?

Coach, halfway out the door, explains, "He told me to find out who Zeno was so that he can share his favorite joke."

And with that, mom burst out laughing. "It's a good one. Until next week then."

Chunk 20:

Building Culture
One Joke at a Time

*F*or Alfred, figuring out the job of a culture-builder was harder than anything he had ever done. Alfred wondered if he had picked wrong by agreeing to be Hannah's narrator, but he understood that he was merely trying to be the best friend possible. As he considered his options, there was no going back, so he simply had to come up with a plan that he could believe in.

Alfred had learned from watching Naruto that "Believe it" was a great credo. Alfred used it when he was in a competitive game of chess or struggling to help his friends understand geometry. Now, he could use "Believe it" as a motivator for *Popposites*. He would unlock the mystery of how to help the cast believe they could be successful on stage.

With persistence and the words of Coach in the back of Alfred's mind, Alfred had begun his job of culture-building—one joke and one moment at a time.

Coach: Hello Alfred! It's good to see you. You left me so curious last time—having to learn about Zeno in anticipation of a nerdy joke.

Alfred: Well, we'll have to come back to that. First, I want to discuss how we used humor to create fun—at least kind of. Then we're onto a tougher topic—how I can maybe help my friends feel successful. You're a lot better at that one.

Coach: I wouldn't say that. I'd say I have more experience, but you are really good at taking my words and running them through your "Coach-Alfred" translator so that they mean something to you.

Alfred: Well, back to my experiment with humor—I asked everyone to bring a joke. They did. I'll share some, but don't feel like you have to laugh. They're not that funny. Ok, there's Mike who plays a teacher. His joke went like this.

Knock, knock. Who's there? Mikey. Mikey who? Mikey doesn't fit in the keyhole!

Coach: Ok, not super funny, but we do have the Mikey connection.

Alfred: Right. We then had some chicken cross-the-road-type jokes. Hannah offered this one, which made me wonder whether she was thinking about herself and *Popposites*.

Why did the rooster cross the road? Because he wasn't chicken.

And Shamisu, who dances in *Popposites*, gave us this:

Why did the fish cross the ocean? To get to the other side.

Coach: Again, not really funny, but maybe humor is in the eye of the beholder. Was it working?

Alfred: Not clear, but everyone did bring a joke. Joey told a light bulb joke which totally fits because he is our stage guy.

How many jugglers does it take to change a light bulb?
One, but it takes at least three light bulbs.

Coach: I'm getting the feel. Well, Rome wasn't built in a day, and culture isn't either. Did you bring a joke?

Alfred: Yes, but mine was a bit hard to get. Let's save that for the end. I want to discuss how to best help my friends so they can feel successful.

Coach: Sure. I can see you are very focused.

Alfred: Coach, I have once a week to pick your brain. I'm making our minutes count. You know… those teaspoonfuls of coffee.

Coach: Def, and by saying that, I've taken out some syllables to save time.

Alfred: And replaced them with many more words. No matter. So, continuing on, I suggested to Hannah that she keep the narrator on stage for the whole show.

Coach: What'd she say?

Alfred: Well, you know it's really not my preference— being on stage the whole time. I just think it'll work best. That way, I can quietly feed people their lines if they forget. Hannah agrees.

Coach: Great.

Alfred: But I want them to mostly not need me. So, I was thinking back to when I couldn't remember people's names. Do you remember what I did?

Coach: You wrote names on your hand.

Alfred: Ding, ding, ding. Color-coded for importance. I'm going to suggest they write a word or two for the tricky parts. Sometimes you only need a small hint to get going.

Coach: Another good idea.

Alfred: I know. Thank you. I probably should have reversed that and said thank you first.

Coach: You're talking to me, Alfred. Be real.

Alfred: Thanks. So, my last "success suggestion" is to change their attitude.

Coach: And by that, you mean?

Alfred: I'm borrowing from our talk about fearing failure.

Coach: Yes. We imagine the worst, and frequently what we're scared of never happens.

Alfred: Yes, so I need my friends to think, "What's the worst that can happen if I forget my lines? Or if I trip on stage? Or maybe I speak over someone else?" There are a million ways to screw up. If you're that nervous person, the whole time, you're thinking, "Everyone is watching me."

Coach: I'm getting nervous just listening.

Alfred: But what if we convince ourselves that our mistakes are just a laugh we didn't plan for? Kind of a *popposite*, which is the point of the whole play?

Coach: You're sounding very wise.

Alfred: You know that I use Hannah to bounce off my ideas. When I told her I wanted to create more laughter, she walked on stage the next day holding two eggs that covered her eyes and asked us, "Who knows what day eggs hate most?" The answer? Fry-day. I knew then that I had her support. She provided us a laugh that we didn't plan for.

Coach: Before we go, is there time for Zeno?

Alfred: Actually, I want to set you up for success too. Let's start with something easier. It's another light bulb joke. Here goes:

How many Einsteins does it take to change a light bulb?

That depends on the speed of the change and the mass of the bulb. But it just might be easier to leave the bulb and change the room. It's all relative.

Coach: Got it. But you did make me think.

Alfred: That might have been the problem when I told the cast. It was a funny failure that I didn't plan for. Coach, I think it's a wrap. I'll keep working on culture. You learn about Zeno.

Coach checks in with Alfred's mom. "Today, I had to work hard to keep up with Alfred. He gives 'focus' new meaning."

"I know he had jokes on his mind and tested quite a few on me. Did he share the Zeno joke with you yet?"

"Not yet. Alfred says that I need to work up to it, so instead, he shared an Einstein joke because, and I quote, 'Coach, I want to set you up for success.'"

"Oh my! Don't we say, 'be careful what you wish for?' He's turned into you. Lucky me!"

"Since you are literal, like Alfred, I am going to assume that you mean it," Coach says with a smile.

"You know that I do. Coach and Alfred are becoming my favorite twofer. Maybe next week Alfred will share the Zeno joke. And you'll have two of us to explain it in case you're confused."

Chunk 21:

Are There Some Soho Globs in the House?

*A*lfred is struggling with the unexpected as Hannah changes plans. He is also working on trying to reduce stress among the cast. Culture-building turns out to be hard work. Alfred wonders whether Soho Globs will dispel his angst. Maybe it's just what the doctor ordered.

Coach: Howdy Alfred! How goes it today?

Alfred: Good—that is if I don't care that nothing is as it should be. Hannah is changing the plan on me and not in a good way.

Coach: What does that mean exactly?

Alfred: Now I need to learn some dance steps. I've also been asked to sing as part of the chorus. And I've still got my narrator role. That feels like a lot for a person who didn't want to even be in *Popposites*.

Coach: Yes, it is. It shows you—and of course Hannah—what a good friend you can be.

Alfred: Only I didn't intend to be this good a friend.

Coach: Well, we've never talked about how we deal with the unexpected—like Hannah's changing the plan. It's hard. We like to be in control, and then whoosh, something gets thrown at us.

Alfred: Yep! In this case, I just got Justin Verlander's fastball. Verlander is a really great pitcher, but you probably knew that.

Coach: Nope, I didn't. Do you see how teaching goes two ways? Anyway, we all struggle with the unexpected.

Alfred: Any ideas on what I can do so that my mood doesn't sink our humor? The cast is trending positive, and I want to keep it that way.

Coach: My advice will sound silly: Expect the unexpected. Then you won't be surprised.

Alfred: That more than "sounds" silly. On a scale of one to ten, it's a one for being helpful.

Coach: Ok. Try this. Look at how far you've traveled. You've got generosity, humor, managing your know-betterer instincts, and facing the fear of failure—all under your belt. You can totally handle a curveball—or maybe a fastball, as you say.

Alfred: So it comes down to just believing in myself?

Coach: Yes, "just." You are bigger than anything thrown at you.

Alfred: For the record, you've never seen me try to dance or sing. Both of those might be bigger. I guess that if I mouth the words, I only have a dance problem.

Coach: Use your smarts to tackle this. I have one other idea, which might hit zero on your helpful scale.

Alfred: As you say, "shoot."

Coach: When I was your age, and something would upset me, my grandma would say, "Put it in your big toe." By that, she meant I should park those thoughts elsewhere and focus on things that matter.

Alfred: You're right. You really have zeroed out on the helpful scale.

Coach: Alfred, use your Coach-Alfred translator to give meaning to my words. And when you do, please let me know what you take from my "big toe" strategy.

Alfred: Not to be mean, but it's just possible that it fails the Coach-Alfred translator, and that "big toe" isn't helpful at all.

Coach: Maybe. You'll report back. But on the topic of the unexpected, I have something else coming your way. I need to be away for two weeks, but I've got a plan.

Alfred: Talk about throwing a fast ball! You know, all week long, I collect crazy moments, and then I say to myself, "Wait until I tell

Coach." Now, what will I do?

Coach: It's only two weeks, and I have a plan.

Alfred: Which is?

Coach: For one of those weeks, I'd like you to write a letter to yourself about what you've figured out over the last year and what you'd like to figure out. This will be helpful.

Alfred: That's it? Does it include figuring out what "put it your big toe" means?

Coach: There's more, and it's ok if my "big toe" strategy doesn't make sense to you. It will someday. For the second assignment, I'd like you to have a significant talk with someone. It could be your mom, Hannah, Mitchell—anyone that matters to you.

Alfred: About what?

Coach: You get to pick, but the important thing is that it is a candid conversation—one that has length and depth—and shares something important to you both.

Alfred: Do I report back?

Coach: That will be up to you.

Alfred: Ok. I think I've reached my limit, but I want to leave you with the Zeno joke I promised. Zeno, as you know from doing your homework, was an ancient mathematician, and one of his ideas was about an infinite series. So, for example, Zeno walks into a school toward the principal's office. He walks half the original distance. Then he walks again, half of the distance. He actually never gets there.

Coach: Using the humor meter, you've just zeroed out.

Alfred: But I've only explained who Zeno is. Now comes the joke. We're back to light bulbs. How many Zenos does it take to change a light bulb?

Coach: I don't know. I'll guess, "an infinite number?"

Alfred: Very good. Yes, infinite. One to screw it in halfway. One to screw it in half of what's left. Another to screw it in half of what's left. You get the idea?

Coach: Yes. It's hard for me to believe that for this, I waited weeks.

Alfred: Let's close out today using Zeno. There's no walk to the principal's office, no infinite series. You'll be back.

Coach: With you closing us out for the day, you actually are starting to sound like me. You will have to decide if it is a good thing or a bad one. Anyway, see you in a few weeks. I am certain that you will have much to share. I look forward to that.

Coach checks in with Alfred's mom. "I'm going to throw you for a small loop, but we'll be ok. I'll be away for two weeks. My mom is getting up there in age, and I need to visit."

"Two weeks should give you some quality time. We'll miss you. Alfred will really miss you, but we know that you serve many."

"Well, to be precise, my mom has served me for years, and my visit is a gift to me. I left Alfred an assignment—a small warning, though. You might have to fill in and pretend to be me."

"Coach, no one can be you, but I can fill in. And we'll be ok. I wish you strength. Moms need that from their children."

Part 2

Chunk 22:

Talking to Yourself

*W*hile Coach is gone for two weeks, Alfred is left with two assignments: Consider what he has learned from Coach and use that to identify what type of help he'd like next. Alfred must also have a significant conversation with someone of his choosing. Up first: A self-assessment.

Alfred 1: Hello Alfred. We're going to try something different today.

Alfred 2: But you're me. We don't like different. Remember?

Alfred 1: Of course, I remember, but this whole year has been about trying something different. That's why we learned people's names. Coach said that was important.

Alfred 2: Well, he was right.

Alfred 1: I know. But let's go ahead in this unusual conversation with ourself and figure out what we've learned. Grown-ups talk to themselves all the time.

Alfred 2: Mom certainly does. Ok. I'll start. The biggest surprise for me is that friends really do make life better.

Alfred 1: Totally agree. But we should also admit that they take a lot too. We need to laugh even when they're not funny. It all comes at a cost. We have less time for Naruto.

Alfred 2: True but learning people's names was a game changer. You remember what we used to do. We had to wait for someone to look at us and then start talking. It was hard, or at least awkward.

Alfred 1: True. And don't forget that it's nicer for the person hearing their name.

Alfred 2: So on the plus side, we've got friends, activities, and that silly exercise of walking in our friends' shoes when we don't understand them. I don't think the shoe-walking helps so much, but occasionally it comes in handy.

Alfred 1: I did like that we learned easy ways to be generous. Something simple like making Soho Globs is an act of generosity, at least according to Coach.

Alfred 2: And we can make them now ourselves—just not as good as mom.

Alfred 1: And wasn't it great that Coach explained that being generous does not necessarily require money, since we don't have much.

Alfred 2: I forget. Is it generous when we let someone win at chess?

Alfred 1: We're not supposed to just give them the game. We don't play our hardest, but we still compete. Coach said that mostly we need to make them feel good at the end—win or lose.

Alfred 2: Can we talk about what's hard?

Alfred 1: Sure. Shoot. Wow, I'm starting to sound like Coach.

Alfred 2: It's really hard to be a great friend when your friend asks so much.

Alfred 1: You're talking about Hannah and *Popposites*.

Alfred 2: Yes.

Alfred 1: Well, Coach and mom would say that it helps us to grow. Also, we don't have to be good friends with everyone—just with a few like Mitchell or Hannah—the ones we really care about.

Alfred 2: Something else I've noticed, now that we've jumped up a level in math, I prefer the kids we hang out with who aren't in our math class.

Alfred 1: I'm curious why.

Alfred 2: The kids in our math class are all about math, all the time!

Alfred 1: Aren't we that way?

Alfred 2: No. We used to be that way. We still love math. It's still a ten in importance, but so are our friends.

Alfred 1: Whoa! That's a big change.

Alfred 2: Yes, it is. I have a different question. Do we think our relationship with mom has changed since Coach came into our life?

Alfred 1: Yes and no. Yes, because I appreciate her more. It turns out she is right about a lot of things. But no, in that she still is the same mom—making dinner, reminding us to shower and do *all* of our homework. Not just math.

Alfred 2: Well, one thing has changed for me. I want to know more about mom. What was it like being raised by Grandma? And what exactly happened to Grandpa? And of course, there's the thing we never bring up. We had to have had a dad somewhere in the picture. There's so much we don't talk about…and so much we don't know about.

Alfred 1: I know. That last thing is hard for me too, but I don't think about it too much. Only occasionally. Instead, I'm focusing on how I can hear the unspoken, and when I actually figure it out, I am going to help mom too.

Alfred 2: So just to summarize: we're better with friends, happier in general, though we wish our friends asked less of us. We appreciate mom more, but we also want to know more. And Coach has given us some helpful lessons like how to be generous, or funny, or not sound so, so smart.

Alfred I: So what's next? That's what Coach wants to know. Maybe some help with anger. I can get mad at Joey for no good reason. Maybe I need to be less picky. That would probably help. When Mitchell gives me his strawberries, and they look bruised, I should just smile and say, "Thank you." I don't think I do that. At chess club, maybe I shouldn't expect the best moves and be happy with "ok" moves. Maybe I should just notice less.

Alfred 2: But Alfred, that's not us. We notice everything.

Alfred I: Ok, so maybe we ask Coach to help us not say all the things we notice. Also, we need to be able to accept things we think aren't quite right.

Alfred 2: Yes, we've got the "suboptimal problem"—a word we can only use with ourselves. Otherwise, we would definitely sound like a know-betterer.

Alfred I: I think this is a good place for us to stop today.

Alfred 2: If you say so.

Alfred I: We'll ask mom if we can really talk to her and we'll quote Coach— "for a candid and deep conversation." We'll tell her it's our assignment and that we might need a whole hour.

Alfred 2: We can offer her a game of chess or maybe watch an extra episode of *Friends* as a way to say thanks.

Alfred 1: Yes. That would show our generous spirit.

Alfred 2: One last thing.

Alfred 1: Yes?

Alfred 2: Can we end with a joke? I'd like to build more humor skills. We're still weak there.

Alfred 1: Sure. Do I need to go first?

Alfred 2: Yes, and I'll be the appreciator.

Alfred 1: Ok. What has ears but cannot hear?

Alfred 2: What?

Alfred 1: A cornfield.

Alfred 2: That's funny—especially for us. Ok, my turn. Why did the teddy bear say no to Soho Globs?

Alfred 1: No one says no to Soho Globs, but why?

Alfred 2: Because she was stuffed.

Alfred 1: All right. We were almost funny, so now it's time to call it a day.

Alfred 2: It's really not that bad—talking to yourself. Thanks, Alfred.

Chunk 23:

A Heart-to-Heart with Mom

𝒜lfred is completing part two of Coach's requirement to have a deeply honest conversation with a person of his choosing. Mom nervously awaits and wonders what is coming her way.

Alfred: Hey, Mom! Thank you for doing this. Coach thanks you too. Hopefully, it will be good for both of us, and you will be happy that I picked you to have a deep and candid conversation with. I'm following Coach's orders.

Mom: Alfred, I am happy to talk to you, even though I think we talk all the time.

Alfred: Well, yes and no. Yes, we talk. "Alfred, did you shower? Alfred, I just made a fresh batch of Soho Globs." But I realize now that there are a lot of things that we don't talk about.

Mom: Such as?

Alfred: I think I'll go easy. After all, I don't want to scare you. So… I want to know what it felt like for you to be raised by Grandma. You can follow that with what exactly happened to Grandpa? And, finally, did you ever wish you had a sister or brother? I know that I do.

Mom: Wow, if that's going easy, I hate to see what going hard would be. You have definitely learned from Coach how to go deep. So, where should I start?

Alfred: If I say, "at the beginning," I might sound like a know-betterer or someone trying to be funny. So start where you want.

Mom: How it felt to be raised by Grandma— lonely. Grandma was dedicated, full of love, and she created a stable home. But there wasn't much fun or laughter. I think she probably fought depression though I don't actually know that.

Alfred: Why do you think that?

Mom: It's tied to your second question about Grandpa. Grandpa and Grandma didn't have a happy marriage. They actually separated for a while, which was rare back then. I would visit Grandpa on Sundays. Then two years after they separated, they decided to give it another try.

Alfred: Then what?

Mom: Do you know the expression, "Fate dealt a cruel hand?" Before they gave it a go, Grandpa had a heart attack and died. That made Grandma especially sad—seeing as they never had another chance. And they did love each other even though they were very different.

Alfred: How were they different? By the way, I never heard that expression. You and Coach like to use expressions a lot—just so you are aware.

Mom: Expressions can be a shorthand way of saying a lot, but we won't explore that one now. Back to your question about how Grandma and Grandpa were different, Grandma is the serious and responsible type. She focuses on meeting all her obligations before she can relax, which by the way, she never does. Grandpa was the life of the party. He told jokes, would raise a toast, played cards with his friends—you can imagine the type. He didn't worry much about tomorrow. I think Grandma wanted him to accept more responsibility.

Alfred: I can't believe I never knew any of this.

Mom: Well, I haven't advertised it. Is it important to you?

Alfred: Yes. It helps me understand where you get your serious side—which pretty much is all of you.

Mom: You asked me whether I wish I had a sister or brother. The answer is "yes," but I knew it wasn't going to be. So instead, I found comfort in reading books, excelling in math, playing chess with myself—basically anything that didn't require people.

Alfred: Wow, we sound a lot alike, but thankfully I have you to play chess with. And that also explains why you thought Coach was important for me. I could hopefully enjoy people in a way that you couldn't.

Mom: Not "couldn't" but "hadn't," and yes, you are onto something. Now I have a question for you. It's on the lighter side. Do you have a favorite color?

Alfred: Hmm. That's an interesting question. I need to think about it. I like yellow because it reminds me of Naruto. His hair is yellow. Dark brown is a good color because they remind me of globs. I don't like red because I connect that with things being wrong. Do you have a favorite color?

Mom: Yes. I like blue and green. When I was a child, I loved looking at the sky and imagining the shapes of clouds. It made me happy to see the blue background. When I was older, I associated blue with "possibilities." We even have the expression "blue sky," which refers to positive opportunities that await. And there I go—offering you another expression.

Alfred: But you also said, "green." Why?

Mom: Green to me equals growth. Sometimes, when I was looking at the sky, I'd be lying on the grass, and I'd notice clover-leaves, which symbolize good luck. I'd see crocuses and hyacinths coming up. I'd think, "Green things grow."

Alfred: So blue and green helped you feel more positive. They gave you optimism.

Mom: I think so. At some point, I stopped feeling lonely.

Alfred: Do you feel lonely now?

Mom: Not really. Things ended up ok. I've got you. My work. Some friends. Now instead of chess, I play more bridge. I do have a question for you, though.

Alfred: Ok. Technically, I'm supposed to be learning about you, but that doesn't seem fair if my questions are the only ones answered.

Mom: Thank you. You are nothing if not fair. Since you just commented that we are a lot alike, I'm curious whether you see that as good or bad.

Alfred: Talk about going deep. Maybe while I think about my answer, you can tell a joke.

Mom: I don't tell jokes well.

Alfred: You need Coach's lesson about humor. Humor is actually within our reach. Ok, I can answer your question. The are many ways that I like that we are so similar. We're smart. I can say that to you and not feel like a show-off. We both like numbers, and we both need time by ourselves. We were both raised by a mom. So that's what I think about our similarities. But we're also different.

Mom: How so?

Alfred: Because of you, I am learning about adding people to my life. I've got chess club, *Popposites,* and I'm even a "culture builder." I don't think you had that growing up. You probably didn't have a mom who understood why it's good to have friends—even when you probably thought you were fine as is. "In summary"—I've learned to finish my essays in school by using those words—I am luckier than you because I have you as my mom.

Mom: Alfred, you have just made me tear up. Thank you. You are honest and very thoughtful. Can we play a game of chess now? I know you have more questions, and I promise to answer them, but I need a break.

Alfred: Yes. My chess game is better now that Mitchell has given me new strategies. You might be in for a loss. Plus, I am better now at hearing unspoken words, so I might read you better.

Mom: I stand warned. By the way, do you know the chess motto? It's, "We are one people." I think it was made for us.

Chapter 24:
The Glass Half-Full

Coach is back from two weeks away and is curious how Alfred did and whether he completed his assignments. Alfred is definitely ready to share what he discovered.

Alfred: Hello, Coach! Boy, have I missed you.

Coach: I can tell because you greeted me before I had a chance to say, "Hello Alfred! Glad I'm back."

Alfred: Well, maybe we both missed each other. Anyway, we have a lot to cover and never enough time. Let's get started.

Coach: Ok. What first—since you seem to be taking the lead?

Alfred: First, I want to say that you look a little tired. I hope you're ok. Moms can take a lot out of us. I know.

Coach: Yes, you're right, but they give a lot too.

Alfred: Well, unless you want to say something more, let's start with my first assignment.

Coach: I don't need to say anything more now that you can read the unspoken word.

Alfred: I'm working on it—or as my mom says, "It's a work in progress." So, you asked me to think about what I've learned from our time together and also what should be next. To do this, I had to talk to myself. Do you ever do that?

Coach: All the time. It appears I am the best at hearing me.

Alfred: I'm pretty good at hearing you too. Anyway, I thought about all that I've learned—walking in my friends' shoes, appearing to know less than I actually do, using humor to change the mood. They're all good lessons, but I need help for when I get stuck. This happens sometimes.

Coach: Stuck? I haven't heard you say that before.

Alfred: "Stuck" mostly happens when I can't change my own mood. So when Joey repeats a stupid chess move or Hannah assumes I will say "yes" to everything, I get irritated. And then it's hard to change my mood.

Coach: You've picked a great next challenge for us to work on: how to "unstick" ourselves.

Alfred: It's only great if we can fix it.

Coach: Well, you've identified the problem, and now we get to figure out a solution.

Alfred: Coach, the way I see it—identifying problems is not a big deal. But help on the way—that's huge!!!

Coach: I didn't say "on the way." You're going to have to work for it.

Alfred: Yes, I know that nothing worthwhile comes easy.

Coach: A good start with un-sticking ourselves is to identify something positive—even if that is not our current mood. Take Joey as an example. What do you appreciate about him?

Alfred: Joey is always there when you need him. He's loyal. He's good at fixing things—which I'm not.

Coach: Then start there the next time you find yourself angry with Joey. An expression that explains what adults often seek is having "A balanced view." In a balanced view, you will see Joey for what he brings and also what he doesn't. How about Hannah?

Alfred: Hannah is smart and sometimes funny. But she just assumes that she gets to make all the decisions. She doesn't.

Coach: Is she a good friend to you?

Alfred: Very good. I could ask her to do something big, and she would do it without complaining.

Coach: So maybe she asks a lot because she gives a lot. Nothing is wrong with that equation.

Alfred: That's not a great use of the word "equation," but I get your point. I should remember the positives. Maybe it's another version of *Popposites*. They both have negatives that bother me, but their positives might be stronger—or at least offer a different angle.

Coach: Angle?

Alfred: Yes, see what you've done! You've got me using math terms in non-math ways which as you know, I don't prefer.

Coach: Sorry, but getting back to the positives and the negatives, I think the two are often related. Maybe Joey is simpler than you in how he sees the world, but he gives in the purest of ways. Maybe Hannah is generous and demanding because everything comes in big amounts for her.

Alfred: I'll need to think about this. Should I rate this advice right now?

Coach: Sure. I'm always interested in whether my words make sense.

Alfred: Remember, I'm a tough scorer. On our one to ten scale, it's a seven in being understandable. However, it might touch a ten in importance. We'll need to see.

Coach: Wow! Love those scores. Maybe a simpler way of making my point is to suggest that you look at the glass half full. It can make you happier.

Alfred: For me, it's not difficult to identify "half-full." What's difficult is letting go of the little things that irritate me—like the way Hannah walks into a room when she has an idea, and she's sure it's a winner. Her confidence can be overwhelming.

Coach: Well, work on it. You'll get there. Now we started today with your telling me that I look tired. I am. I've just spent two weeks with one of the most important people in my world. Alfred, today's conversation helps me. My mom is getting older. She doesn't remember as much. Her energy and curiosity come in occasional spurts.

Alfred: That must be really hard.

Coach: It is, but applying the glass half-full approach, I need to appreciate what she still gives me. During her spurts, she's as wise and funny as ever.

Alfred: Does your mom have a sense of humor?

Coach: Where do you think I learned to appreciate humor? It's all mom.

Alfred: Well, we won't have time today to discuss my super interesting conversation with my mom—our second assignment. But it seems like we both have good reasons to appreciate our moms.

Coach: Yes, we do, and your mom even comes with Soho Globs.

Alfred: Just curious, does your mom make globs?

Coach: Nope.

Alfred: Maybe I can make her some. She should know how they taste.

Coach: You are very kind, and she'd love them. So since you started us off, where do we go next, Alfred?

Alfred: I am going to work on seeing the "glass-half-full." Being literal, if I fill my glass with milk and eat a glob, the lesson will stick. When I see Joey, I'll think "loyal." "When I see Hannah, I'll think "big giver." When my mom irritates me, I'll change lessons and remember your saying to "walk in someone's shoes."

Coach: You're both versatile and spot on in deciding what to do with whom. Way to incorporate our lessons, Alfred!

Alfred: My moves can be awkward, but I will report back, and I will also make some globs for you to send your mom. She sounds like she deserves them.

Coach: She does. See you next week.

It's been awhile since Coach dropped in on Alfred's mom. "You doing ok, Eleanor?"

"Coach, it's good to see you, and yes, we're doing well. Alfred and I had a great chat last week—the first of its kind. But I'm going to let him share it with you."

"That's smart and also very respectful of Alfred. It's funny that in my two weeks away, I see Alfred's growth. It makes me wonder how much longer I'll be needed."

"Oh, please don't wonder. We need you for the duration. And I want to emphasize, 'we.'"

"Ok, then. We'll leave it at that. See you next week."

Chunk 25:

All Moms are Alike—or Are They?

Alfred is prepared to share with Coach his second assignment, which was to engage in one deep and candid conversation. Alfred left the conversation with his mom wanting to ask more questions, but he also understood that his mom was fatigued and needed a break. Maybe Coach can add some perspective.

Coach: Good afternoon, Alfred. I think I'll put myself at the helm today.

Alfred: You're the boss. You get to choose.

Coach: Now Alfred, we know I'm not the boss. Who is?

Alfred: Great lead-in to my update! We know who's the boss. It's our moms, and because of that, I brought you something—for later.

Coach: Moms it is. And thank you. So about those moms of ours, why go there?

Alfred: Because that was who I chose for a long and kind of scary conversation. I learned a lot. I don't know why it took me so long to ask some obvious questions. And of course, there were questions I didn't ask, but I won't forget those when there is a next time.

Coach: You might have waited because you weren't quite ready to hear the answers. And it sounds like there are more answers you'd like.

Alfred: Yes, that's true, but let's start with a question that is a good intro to my mom's and my conversation. Do you know your mom's favorite color?

Coach: Not really. Or at least, I've never asked.

Alfred: Me neither, but my mom asked me. It tells you something.

Coach: How so?

Alfred: My mom's favorite color is actually "colors," and it's blue and green. Do you know why?

Coach: How could I possibly know? That's a rhetorical question. I can explain that later if you don't know what 'rhetorical' means.

Alfred: I'd rather focus on why colors matter. When my mom was growing up, she spent a lot of time by herself. Grandpa and Grandma didn't get along. Grandma might have been depressed. My mom had to learn to entertain herself. She played chess by herself. She read a lot of books. And she would lie on the grass and look at the clouds and identify their shapes. She said that looking at the blue sky made her happy because it felt so positive. She also looked at the grass and things growing—like 4-leaf clovers. For her, blue and green meant happy and growing.

Coach: Alfred, what you just shared is deeply moving. It says a lot about the strength and resilience of your mom. I think she has passed that on to you.

Alfred: Well, it definitely makes me appreciate her differently. I never thought about her being lonely as a kid. So do you think your mom has a favorite color?

Coach: Well, she wears a lot of purples, so I think I'd go with that. Purple feels like a color that says, "I'm here!" My mom is no shrinking violet—pun intended—so I think purple suits her.

Alfred: I've got another question.

Coach: OK, but it seems like we've switched seats again, and you're back in charge.

Alfred: Now Coach, we've just decided it's our moms who are really in charge. So second question: What was your mom's favorite TV show?

Coach: I've got to think for a second. Do you have an answer?

Alfred: Yep, this one's easy. *Friends.* I have watched so many episodes with her. It's one of the ways I feel generous. Only now I understand why she keeps coming back to a series whose lines she knows by heart. It's a world of friends—the one she never had. People share stories, jokes, unhappy moments, food, everything!!! It must make her feel warm—like she is practically there.

Coach: OK, I know my answer. My mom loved the *Mary Tyler Moore Show*, which was before your time. I think I can explain why too. Mary Tyler Moore was a woman building a profession. She was out in the world, exploring, working. We take that for granted today, but not when my mom was raising me.

Alfred: So look at what that one question shows us. My mom missed having friends. Your mom missed work. Add to that our question about colors. My mom needed something positive. Your mom was looking to stand out. In many ways, our moms are similar—trying to fill a hole, doing their best to raise us. But they are also very different. My mom plays chess, makes globs, and likes her quiet. Not sure what your mom does.

Coach: My mom volunteered at church. She helped out at "nursing homes"—what we'd call senior centers now. She cared for people who needed something extra.

Alfred: That sounds like you. One more super interesting thing that I learned. My grandma was very serious, making sure they had a home and food—the things we all need. My grandpa was a guy who didn't like to worry. He wanted to have fun—play cards, have a drink with the guys. They eventually separated. Now I know where my mom gets her serious side—which I told her is pretty much all of her. That's probably why we're not so good at humor. But I'm learning—thanks to you.

Coach: And to think that all I asked of you is to have one honest and revealing conversation, and here is where you landed.

Alfred: I know, and I'm not done. I have more questions, but she was getting tired, and we decided to take a break and finish another time. So instead, we played chess. But I just know that there's more ahead.

Coach: I'm proud of you. You show guts, and honesty, and a healthy curiosity. And you read people—at least your mom—so well. You stopped when you needed to.

Alfred: Changing topics, I've made these Soho Globs. Can you send them to your mom? I wrote her a note to go with it.

Coach: Sure.

Alfred: Feel free to read the note—now if you want.

Coach: (reading) *"Dear Coach's mom, I don't know you, but I know your son. He has helped me a lot. Thank you for doing a very good job being his mom. In that way, you have helped us both. Signed, Alfred"*

Alfred: OK, Coach, gotta go. We are having a *Popposites* rehearsal—more on that next week. I'll come up with an assignment, including my favorite color and why. Maybe you can give it some thought too. Bye.

Coach stops in to say hi to Eleanor. "To tell you the truth, I don't even know what to say. I was really moved by today's conversation. I need to digest it before I can say anything."

"You've got me curious, but I can wait. I've learned patience."

Coach says as he walks out, "It sounds like you've learned a lot more than that, and you have passed it on to Alfred. Amazing is all I can say. Let's talk more next week when I've had a chance to really process what Alfred just shared."

"See you then," Eleanor says. "I'm not going anywhere."

Chunk 26:

What's in a Color?
(Language Arts Assignment #5)
An Essay by Alfred

I've picked an unusual topic for a creative writing assignment, but there is more to this topic than meets the eye. I have to admit that of the many things I think about, color has never been one of them. That is until my mom asked me what my favorite color was and then explained why blue and green were special to her. She needed symbols of growth and optimism and those colors, which felt like sky and grass to her, did it.

Just that small interaction—well, it wasn't really small because it was the first long and painfully honest conversation that I've had with my mom since chess strategy doesn't really count—has opened my eyes. Yes, I now see that the colors people prefer can be a possible indication of something. This is a small change for me. I usually see my world in terms of numbers, patterns, and statistics, and color does not fall into any of those categories. It belongs in what I call the "soft and squishy basket of emotions," which I am not good at understanding, and until recently, didn't really care about.

My favorite color, as I told my mom was a tie between yellow and brown. I think those are unusual picks, but I have my reasons. What started me thinking yellow was Naruto, who has a fake blondish kind of hair. For a long time now, Naruto was really my only friend. Then Coach came along, and my friendship circle expanded, and now I have brunette, black, and even red-haired friends. This leads me to believe that my reasons for liking yellow have changed.

Now I like yellow because it symbolizes caution—as in "go slowly before proceeding." That is kind of how I've gone after expanding my world: One step at a time, easy does it. Yellow seems to be my speed.

But why brown? Short and simple, nothing makes me happier than eating a Soho Glob while watching Naruto. Soho Globs are rich chocolate cookies with a perfect texture, and unless you've tasted one, you might just say, "Oh, so just a chocolate cookie!" Wrong! It's not just another chocolate cookie—it's special.

Maybe the color brown is a symbol to me, just like the color yellow is. I think that often what's on the surface does not really tell you what's inside. One bite into a glob, and you know it's different. I am different too. On the surface, I might seem like your average kid, only a little more awkward (I used to be a lot more awkward). My height, weight, hair color, and face do not make me special. But what's inside might. At least that is what I am betting on though I haven't figured out the odds yet.

And so now I understand what's in a color.

Chunk 27:

Understanding Another Side

*C*oach and Alfred are meeting with no clear assignment though Alfred said he'd figure something out, and he has.

Alfred: Hey, Coach. Our meeting might be a little different today. I said I'd figure out something worthwhile, and I have.

Coach: Great. You've got me curious. I'm all ears, as they say.

Alfred: Do you remember how you said I needed to look at the glass half-full? As relates to Joey, instead of getting frustrated that he's not getting better at chess, you said to think about his other side—you know, the good loyal friend who can fix anything.

Coach: Yes, I remember that.

Alfred: So when I left you last week, I was heading to a *Popposites* rehearsal. It was a good one. Then as we left the building, one of our friends, Shamisu, a dancer in the play, was going to head home on her bike. Only her bike didn't work. And there was no one for Shamisu to call to pick her up. She started crying.

Coach: So let me guess—Joey to the rescue.

Alfred: You're so smart—maybe not with numbers, but definitely with people.

Coach: Small interruption first. You don't know that I'm not good with numbers. You just assume. That would be like someone assuming you are not good with people. But you are.

Alfred: I am? Thank you! I'll take it. Anyway, Joey came out with his tools, which he carries in his backpack—just in case they're needed. Have you ever heard of someone carrying around an Allen wrench just in case? Until last week, I would have said an Allen wrench is a wrench that belongs to person named Allen. But it's actually a specific tool.

Coach: Yes, I know.

Alfred: Well, I didn't. Anyway, Joey goes out there. He's calm. He has his tools. He is very serious—he has the look that I probably have when I'm trying to solve a hard math problem. He takes off the wheels, the bike chain, and a bunch of other stuff. He gets out his Allen wrench, and before you know it, we have a working bike. He was like a grown-up in how he handled the moment.

Coach: So I take it your view of Joey has changed.

Alfred: Definitely, and as I was getting ready to tell him what a great job he did, he said he had to hurry home and walk his dog, "Calvin." I didn't even know he had a dog.

Coach: Did it matter to you that he had a dog?

Alfred: Only in that it got me curious—how big, how friendly, how old, and a bunch of other questions.

Coach: I'm guessing you'll have the opportunity.

Alfred: Oh, I will! But my list is growing of people I want to have long conversations with. There's my mom. Now Joey. At some point, Grandma. There are so far three people on my list, and this is coming from a person who doesn't even like to talk that much! You know me—quiet time with globs and Naruto equal heaven.

Coach: You can actually like both—conversation and lone time. They are not mutually exclusive. But back to Joey, what did you learn?

Alfred: Well, you said earlier not to assume things—like you and your skill with numbers. It's true with Joey too. He's smart in a different way. And mostly, he's so happy to be helpful—to everyone! And he doesn't brag about it. He just does it. I like that.

Coach: Does that translate into respect?

Alfred: Completely. He is becoming one of my favorite friends. And I'm going to ask him to teach me about dogs. Maybe someday, if I like dogs, I can convince my mom that we should get one. It could be good for both of us. It won't replace having a sister or brother, but it would probably help. But first, I need to learn more.

Coach: So, what did this week's self-assigned assignment teach you? By the way, it's kind of funny to hear "self-assigned assignment." I'm wondering if you can hear why it's funny.

Alfred: I can hear it. It's more like words that repeat themselves, making a joke. Anyway, to answer your question about what I learned, it might be cheating to work backward, but this is how I see it. I tried to practice what you call "the glass half-full" and see Joey differently. I tried not to let little details get in the way—like how he always brings out his queen too soon. And guess what?

Coach: What?

Alfred: I was able to see him differently.

Coach: Isn't an open mind a wonderful thing?

Alfred: Yes, especially if—and I don't know this is the case—but maybe one day I might convince my mom that a dog should be in our life. She would need an open mind.

Coach: So I think there is one more lesson from this last week of yours.

Alfred: Now you've got me curious.

Coach: Identifying our assumptions and then challenging them.

Alfred: Really good point, Coach. People assume I am smart and have all the answers. I couldn't have told you that an Allen wrench is not a tool belonging to Allen.

Coach: Now it's my turn to give you the assignment.

Alfred: As you say, "shoot."

Coach: I want you to identify three assumptions in your life that are worth challenging.

Alfred: Ok. But before I leave, did you ever come up with a color that you really like? You don't know this, but I even wrote an essay for my Language Arts class on colors and what they mean. I hope you found some color that means something to you.

Coach: I thought about it. The short answer is no. I seem to be color-less. But I have an affirmative longer answer for a show that I love. You asked me that question too. Kind of like a twofer to use your language. I love *The Big Bang Theory*. It's like *Friends* in that you have a mix of people who share their life—disappointments, hopes, games, food, and even the strangeness of their families. We all have 'em. But there is a "smart" side to characters like Sheldon that I really enjoy. And Sheldon grows so much.

Alfred: All right, it sounds like I need to suggest to my mom that we try out *The Big Bang Theory*. If you want, you can leave your mind open about the question of color. Something might come to you. Since you're teaching me about an open mind, it's a chance for you to demonstrate that you've got one too *(laughing)*.

Coach: Ok, I'll give it some thought, but if there is an answer out there, it's not obvious. And that might be a lesson in itself—how different we are in what we connect with. Stew on that!

Alfred: I will. By the way, I've never heard "stew on that," but I understand it anyway. Now that I've got my assignment—to challenge three assumptions—I gotta go. I am talking to Mitchell and Hannah about chess club and whether we can start a small tournament. We need to figure out whether people will feel good at the end or feel defeated. See you next week.

Coach stops by to say hi to Alfred's mom. "Today, the topic was keeping an open mind and challenging our assumptions."

Alfred's mom gives a big smile. "That's hard for us adults, let alone our kids."

"Well, it might become particularly hard for you depending on where Alfred takes his 'open mind.' Consider yourself forewarned."

"That only helps a bit since I don't know what I am being forewarned about. Will I see you next week?"

Coach nodded yes as he headed out the door. He was reminding himself, "The blessings of an open mind."

Chunk 28:

Alfred and Joey Talk Dogs

*A*lfred left last week's meeting with Coach intent on learning more about dogs. It fit right into Coach's assignment for Alfred to challenge some assumptions. Just for starters, why did Calvin seem so important to Joey? Is there more to dogs than meets the eye? His curiosity piqued, and Coach's assignment on his mind, Alfred has asked Joey if he can join him after school to walk Calvin.

Alfred: Joey, thanks for letting me come along. I've never walked a dog before—well, technically, I am not walking the dog. You are.

Joey: I do this every day. Actually, I do this twice a day—once in the morning before going to school and later when I get home.

Alfred: So first I want to know, what kind of dog is Calvin?

Joey: America's most popular breed— a Labrador retriever. I assume you know what "breed" is.

Alfred: Yes, I know the word "breed." Is it really America's most popular breed, or are you just saying it? And if it is, why? And who is number two?

Joey: I don't know for sure, but that's what they say, so I think it's true. Why labs are so liked is because they are simple, loyal dogs that love to fetch balls and be with their owner. They're smart enough to be trained but not too smart, which is good. Dogs that are too smart can be harder to handle. I'm guessing the second most popular breed is a golden retriever. Alfred, is there anything that you don't like data on?

Alfred: I don't think so, but you're doing great. So how often does Calvin eat? Did you have to work hard to convince your mom to get a dog? Can you tell if Calvin is sad? There's more.

Joey: Whoa! Ok, I'll try to answer these. Calvin eats twice a day— one and one-half cups of kibble, which is what you call dry dog food. My mom grew up with a lab, so she wanted one because she knows how it feels to have a dog keep you company. To read Calvin's mood, I look at his tail. If it is tucked low between his legs and down, it usually means something is scaring him. If it is up and straight, like a windshield wiper, he's on alert. If it is loose and wagging, he's happy.

Alfred: So it's all in the tail?

Joey: Kind of. His face can sometimes tell me something. His eyes can read sparkly, sad, or flat and tired.

Alfred: What's the hardest thing about having a dog?

Joey: Sometimes, you have to put their needs before yours. Like if I want to stay late at school, I need to think about how long because Calvin needs to get out—both to pee or poop and to run after a ball. By the way, dog owners frequently say, "My dog has to do business," instead of using the word "poop," but don't ask me why.

Alfred: Ok, I'll resist though you've got me curious how "business" relates to "poop." Here is an easy question though. What's the best thing about having a dog?

Joey: They love you like nothing else ever does. You are God to them. They are so loyal, and they only see you as great. I sometimes need to be seen as great—because I know I'm not.

Alfred: Actually, I think you're great. It took me a while, but now I know. You're very helpful to practically everyone. You are what my mom calls "handy." You can fix everything. And here you are, answering all of my questions patiently, too. I still have more, though, so you're not done.

Joey: That's ok. I'm happy to share something I know about.

Alfred: Do dogs smell?

Joey: Definitely. When they get wet, which labs do any chance they can because they love water, labs get a "wet dog smell." And their breath is a whole 'nother matter. You are supposed to brush their teeth, but we don't do that so much, and then our vet gets mad when he sees Calvin's teeth.

Alfred: You are supposed to brush with toothpaste?

Joey: Yes, it comes in chicken flavored, but I don't recommend you try it. Some people use "greenies" instead, which are shaped like dog bones. It's easier because dogs eat them, and supposedly their teeth are cleaner, but I don't think they work as well as brushing.

Alfred: Joey, are you noticing right now that Calvin is eating dirt?

Joey: Yep. He does it all the time. Dogs do that. Don't worry.

Alfred: Ok, I'm going to trust you on this, but it's not obvious that I shouldn't worry. Also, you keep on throwing the ball with that stick. Doesn't Calvin get tired? I am getting tired just watching you both.

Joey: It's called a "chuck-it," and Calvin gets excited when he sees it because he knows there's some fun ahead. The chuck-it helps me throw the ball much further, and Calvin needs the exercise. Otherwise, he'll get fat. Most labs do. I'm trying hard to see that it doesn't happen to Calvin.

Alfred: Hypothetically speaking, and this is very hypothetical if I get a dog—or rather if I am able to convince my mom that a dog would be great in our life—would you help me train him or her? Not sure which.

Joey: Sure, but it takes a long time to understand dogs, and it's not so easy to train a puppy. It's not super hard, but you have to keep at it. Also, there are things you need to be careful about.

Alfred: Such as?

Joey: Well, I know that you love those chocolate cookies. I think you call them Soho Globs. Right? Anything with chocolate is very dangerous for dogs. Grapes and raisins—same thing. So, you need to keep those things out of reach. Also, when you first train a puppy, you just know there are going to be accidents in the house. Usually, people keep their puppy in a fenced-off area so that they can keep the mess in one space.

Alfred: This is so helpful, and nothing you've said has scared me off. It probably would scare my mom, though. I have to admit that it makes me sad that I could never share my favorite cookie with a puppy—the one we might never get. My sadness might just be entirely theoretical.

Joey: Well, just so you know, there are a ton of treats you can give dogs—beef, lamb, chicken, salmon flavored. And there's peanut butter-based treats. You and the hypothetical puppy would be fine.

Alfred: Thanks, Joey. That is very helpful.

Joey: Alfred, I'm here if you have more questions. I gotta head home, feed Calvin, and then do some homework. Homework doesn't come as easy for me as it does for you.

Alfred: Well, I can help you with your homework if you need it. My offer stands, even if we don't get a dog. I'm going to be just like you—happy to help.

Joey: Thank you. That's really nice. See you tomorrow.

Chunk 29:

Float Like a Butterfly: Alfred Chooses His Style

*A*fter taking a walk with Joey, Alfred can't shake his desire to add a dog to his life. He has decided to broach the topic with his mom. He's not sure how, but he knows that he needs to proceed ahead carefully. "After all," Alfred tells himself, "Life is all about having an open mind—That's what my mom told me when she wanted Coach to be part of my life, and it's what Coach says to me too. I need to up my chances with my mom. I also need to keep an open mind about her response. It might not be what I want to hear."

Alfred: Mom, I think it's time we had another chat.

Mom: Somehow, when you say that, it makes me nervous. What's up?

Alfred: Nothing much. Whatever you imagine is much worse than anything I could share.

Mom: Ok, so what's today's topic?

Alfred: Did Coach tell you that we are working on challenging our assumptions and keeping an open mind?

Mom: He made a slight reference to it, but he didn't elaborate.

Alfred: For example, Coach just might be better with numbers than I give him credit for, and he says that I am better with people than I give myself credit for.

Mom: Ok, so what are you going to do with that?

Alfred: Great question. I am working on having an open mind, and you'll never guess where my open mind has taken me.

Mom: You're right. I won't. Maybe studying the field of psychology?

Alfred: No. Much simpler than that, but first, some background. I know you've heard me talk about Joey. He's slow at learning chess, good at building the *Popposites'* stage, excellent at fixing a broken bike. Joey's fix-it skills helped Shamisu get home the other day. He's actually great, but it took me a while to realize that.

Mom: Ok.

Alfred: And he has a dog, named Calvin, who I got to meet and go on a walk with yesterday.

Mom: Hmmm. You are a curious person—dogs? Ok, well the world presents us with so much to learn about.

Alfred: And love. Don't forget, it's really, "learn about *and love.*" *(said with emphasis)*

Mom: Ok. So?

Alfred: So, I am thinking that a dog would bring some more love into our home. We'd have chess, eat Soho Globs, watch *Friends* — but we'd have a dog cuddled up next to us.

Mom: Forget psychology, Alfred. I think you've got a future in sales—"cuddled up with a dog watching *Friends.*" Let me catch my breath. I haven't been practicing having an open mind like you have. Frankly, this is a tough one for me to get my arms around.

Alfred: I know. That's the tough thing about having an open mind—an idea you originally planted when the topic of Coach came up. An open mind can take us to places we haven't been—like dogs.

Mom: You don't know much about dogs.

Alfred: Totally true, but I have two things to say. I am a quick learner, and Joey will help me.

Mom: You went on exactly one dog walk. In the world of numbers, is that enough data for you?

Alfred: In the world of numbers, probably not. But with Coach's help, and also a little bit of you, I am adding more than numbers to my life. There are some things that I find valuable with no numbers attached. I can't believe it myself! It's actually an assumption I need to challenge.

Mom: Well, you're not going to get an answer from me today. I need to think about this—you know, consider all the ramifications of possibly having a dog. By the way, there aren't too many kids with whom I can use the word "ramifications" and know they will understand me.

Alfred: You only have one kid, so I think you are ok.

Mom: There is one question I have for you, though. I thought we were doing fine. You are in the process of building a nice group of friends. You've got chess club, *Popposites*, and you can even make your own Soho Globs. Am I right... we're doing fine?

Alfred: Yes, we are, but do you remember a conversation we had when you convinced me to meet with Coach? I said I was fine, and you said that I was more than fine but that I could be even better. Well, that's what I think here. We are fine, but we could be even better.

Mom: Wow, that feels like my words coming right back at me.

Alfred: Because they are.

Mom: Well, in the words of Coach, you've given me my homework assignment. I am going to challenge some assumptions—like not wanting or needing a dog. For you, though, and maybe for Coach, I will commit to keeping an open mind.

Alfred: Thank you. I wasn't sure how hard I should make my case. Do you know the fighter who said, "Float like a butterfly, sting like a bee?"

Mom: Of course. That was Mohammad Ali, and he was way before your time.

Alfred: Yes, but I track sports heroes, and he was huge. Anyway, I love this famous line of his, which I've seen on YouTube, and I love that I finally got to use it. In our case, I have opted to float and not push you too hard. If we get a dog, I want you to be as excited as me.

Mom: Ok, so I think we can stop here. We're good for now.

Alfred: To be more exact, we're "fine," and maybe we're trending towards "better." I will tell Coach that I am proud of how you didn't do a takedown and that you are considering my idea.

Mom: Thanks

Alfred: I won't tell you what other assumptions I am challenging or even what other questions I may have in the back of my mind. I've given you enough to think about.

Mom: Thank you

Alfred: But just so you know, our conversations have the "pig principle" in play.

Mom: I don't think I know the pig principle.

Alfred: Wow, for once, I get to educate you. The pig principle is that when goods are good, you only want more. In our case, because I enjoy our conversations, I will only want more of them.

Mom: Lucky me!

Alfred: Well, I realize that our conversations are helpful and sometimes fun. I usually learn something.

Mom: Ok. I'll take that and the pig principle and say, "Thank you."

Alfred: I hope I didn't leave you thinking, "What did I set into motion when I brought Coach into our lives." You might eventually find our conversations to be a plus for you. It might just take some time.

Mom: Yes, it might just take some time. I wouldn't use the word "fun." It's more like me saying to myself, "Alfred has another surprise in store for me. What unexpected blessing might it be?" And then I add, after a second, "And is it really a blessing?"

Alfred: On that note, I am heading out now to meet Joey and Calvin. I've got a lot to learn, just in case—I won't say any more.

Chunk 30:

Assumptions Gone Wild

*C*oach had asked Alfred to challenge some assumptions and to answer for himself what is the value of having an "open mind." Alfred's discussions with his mom and Joey provide the means and the lesson.

Alfred: I think I'd better be in charge again. Sorry Coach. By the way, how are you?

Coach: I'm not as focused as you, it appears. I think, by the way, that sometimes social amenities —you know, the hi's and how are you's—don't fit the mood. In that instance, it's ok to skip them.

Alfred: Ok. So I had two conversations that made me challenge some assumptions, and then a later conversation at the bottom-of-the-ninth did it again. I'm sure you got the baseball analogy. Anyway, now my mind is so open it feels lost.

Coach: Whoa! The struggles of being Alfred, and yes, I got the analogy.

Alfred: Feeling lost is not a good feeling if you're me, but depending on where I land, all might be good.

Coach: Let's start with the first conversation.

Alfred: Ok. I took a walk with Joey to learn more about Calvin and dogs in general. It was super interesting. Calvin eats dirt, which Joey says is normal for dogs. Calvin chases the ball, brings it back to Joey, and they do this again and again—like twenty times, but I lost count because I was asking questions.

Coach: Was it fun?

Alfred: Totally. We were outdoors, Calvin was happy, and Joey could explain things I knew nothing about. He became my teacher.

Coach: I bet you didn't expect that role reversal.

Alfred: Correct. So right there, I knocked out two assumptions. One—that I wouldn't really like dogs, but maybe I'd only like the idea of them. This proved false. And two—that Joey couldn't teach me anything.

Coach: That's great awareness, and you really learned something. So tell me what happened in your second conversation?

Alfred: I spoke with my mom. Specifically, I asked her about maybe getting a dog.

Coach: I bet she was surprised.

Alfred: Yes, she didn't see that coming. She asked a really good question. Did one single dog walk provide me with enough data to tell me I wanted a dog?

Coach: What'd you say?

Alfred: I told her that you had opened up my mind about data. Data is important, but it doesn't rule everything. It's not one of those ten commandments: "You shall live your life according to data." By the way, Coach, that's my attempt to be funny.

Coach: You actually were, and of course, I appreciate that you believe there is more to life than data.

Alfred: This conversation took me to realizing that I need to challenge the role of data in my life. I mean, until now, I've lived my life with data as my compass, always directing me. That may not be my way in the future.

Coach: Good for you—for realizing this. And just so you know, challenging our assumptions is a lifelong venture. We are never done. So what'd your mom say?

Alfred: Another surprise! She didn't rule it out, but she needs time to think about it. I told her it would be fun to cozy up with a puppy on the sofa while we watched *Friends*, and then she called me a salesman.

Coach: *(laughing)* And how did you leave it?

Alfred: Here, I was proud of myself. Usually, you're the one to say that, but I said it to myself—with unspoken words. I told my mom that I was thinking of the saying, "Float like a butterfly, sting like a bee." Should I argue really hard—the sting approach? Or should I show patience—the float approach—and gently let her find her way to getting a dog? There are risks. We lose time, and she might not say "yes," but I chose to float like a butterfly.

Coach: That was the right approach, very mature. Once again, you show great instincts. Data was not the deciding factor.

Alfred: Yes, but it's left me wondering, "What do I do now?"

Coach: It's like Soho Globs baking in the oven. You wait. You've done your job. You let time take its course.

Alfred: Ok, but globs are much easier. They only take eleven minutes. This will take more. We can let that sit because I have another thing to bring up, and it's making me very sad.

Coach: Yes.

Alfred: You know Hannah has been having a tough time. She is brother-sitting, running *Popposites*, keeping her straight-A record, and even fitting in chess club. Hannah seems stressed and sometimes angry. Anyway, she told me that she and her brother are going to live with their dad this summer in Terre Haute, Indiana, which is two hours away. She said her mom needs a break, and they would probably return, but not definitely.

Coach: She's such a good friend to you.

Alfred: Yes. I was able to hold back tears but barely. She adds so much fun to any room she's in, and very often, I'm in that room with her.

Coach: I don't have much to offer other than whatever the future holds, you and Hannah will stay close friends. You bring her at least as much as she brings you.

Alfred: Thank you for saying that—even if it's not true.

Coach: Oh, but it is. I think it's ok, even good, to sit with that sadness. It will morph into a lot of other emotions. You will learn something and probably even add another layer to your friendship.

Alfred: Ok. I think I'm tired. I think I'll see if Joey is around. Maybe we can walk Calvin again. That would be my third time—I'm on my way to a full dataset!

Coach: Alfred—using the ten commandments was very clever.

Alfred: Thanks. Every once in a while, I can surprise me, and even you. So, what's my assignment?

Coach: You're going to love it. You started with a baseball analogy. I'll finish with one. It's the "Seventh-inning stretch." I want you to relax. Moving from a baseball analogy to the bible, I want you to count your blessings. But just to be clear because we know that you run literal, you don't need to actually count them.

Alfred: Seventh-inning stretch? Count your blessings? Look at you, clever Coach. Who's learning from who? That would be another assumption I could challenge. I thought I was only learning from you, but this may not be the case. I won't "count" my blessings, but I will consider them and report back next week.

Coach checks in with Alfred's mom. "So, I'm guessing Alfred threw you for a loop with talk of a puppy."

"Yes, he did, and I'm still thinking about it. It would probably be good for Alfred—less good for me. I'm digesting what the new reality could look like, but I'm not ready to bite. No pun intended."

"Well, Alfred was impressed with your open mind. How he explained it to me made him sound restrained on the topic. He didn't go for the close."

Mom shrugs, "Yes. He was respectful and kind. If I go where no sane mom dares go, well … I won't finish that sentence. Alfred wants me to be as happy about a dog as he apparently is. But of course, I have years on me which means I bring perspective to the topic."

Coach looks perplexed. "I won't ask you more, but do I need to prepare Alfred for a possible 'no'? I could go down the path of how our experiences shape us."

"No, please don't. I always say, 'TWT,' or time will tell. Let me sit with this for a bit. Alfred seems ok about waiting for a response."

"Yes, he is. He mentioned that."

"But Coach, you know what I won't say?"

"What?"

"I won't say 'thank you for opening our minds' because that is what got us into this mess. Whatever the outcome, only one of us will be happy."

The sound of that made Coach wince. "I hear you, but Eleanor, I don't think we can predict how we'll feel when a new reality hasn't even emerged. You might surprise yourself, just like Alfred has surprised himself in deciding to work with me."

Now there was silence. She did bear some responsibility for the chain of events, and her instincts about what she needed to do for Alfred turned out to be good. She just hadn't understood where all this could lead them.

Coach continued, "You just don't know, and that's the thing about having an open mind. It can create possibilities that we couldn't have imagined, and some of those things are probably beneficial."

Now there was quiet again. Envisioning possibilities took work, and she hadn't done that in years. It also brought back some memories that she had buried so that she could get on with the business of living.

Coach, recognizing the stillness and thought, added in a soft-spoken manner, "Change is bound to happen because of the doors you've opened up for Alfred. You are giving him what you had hoped. His world is richer. There are more people. And there might, or might not be a dog, but we can work with whatever reality you choose."

Eleanor, still looking down, was trying to decipher how different their world—hers and Alfred's—might look in the year ahead. She took a deep breath and looked up. Somehow, if she let go of her fear, maybe it wouldn't be so bad. And then she heard what she needed.

"Whatever happens won't be bigger than you, and I will be around. Alfred will help make this work if that is what you choose. Have faith—both in him and in your ability to adapt."

"Well, it helps to know that you will be around. I have a lot to think about and a mind to open up, and I believe that I will have faith. Let's see where I am next week. We'll talk then."

Chunk 31:

It's Granny Time

*C*oach gave Alfred a "seventh-inning stretch," by which he meant that Alfred should relax. With time on his hands and untamed curiosity, Alfred heads straight to Grandma. One-on-one conversations are now becoming his thing.

Alfred: Grandma, I am so glad to see you. I've realized recently there's a lot that I don't know about you. We should know about the things we love. I don't mean to suggest you're a thing, but mostly that I have a lot of questions.

Grandma: Sure. I feel flattered that you want to know more about me.

Alfred: Well, you say that now, but we will see if you say that later. Just remember, curiosity is another side of love.

Grandma: I'm ready. You don't scare me.

Alfred: Ok. Let's start with Grandpa. Mom told me how you both loved each other but were too different to make it easy to stay married. So you separated, and just when you decided to get back together again, he died. That must have been very hard on you.

Grandma: It was and still is in some ways.

Alfred: If I was that sad, I would sit on the sofa, watch Naruto and eat Soho Globs. But you wouldn't do that. So, what did you do?

Grandma: I cried. I felt angry and lost. And then I realized I had your mom to raise and money that I needed to make so that we would have a roof over our heads and food to eat. I worked as a bookkeeper because I was good with numbers. The job paid well enough.

Alfred: So maybe that's where I got my love of numbers. Maybe I inherited it. Did you talk to anyone about how sad you were feeling? You know I talk to Coach, who is way more helpful than I expected.

Grandma: Back then—over thirty years ago—it wasn't so common to talk to someone. No, I just "gutted it out," as they say.

Alfred: I don't know that saying, but it makes me think of fish—and not in a good way.

Grandma: It has nothing to do with fish. I put my head down and toughened up. I woke up each morning and put one foot in front of the other. I'd get your mom off to school and head straight to work.

Alfred: Do you remember the first time you laughed after Grandpa died?

Grandma: Funny you should ask because I do. Your mom had come home from school. She was rehearsing her lines in The Wizard of Oz. She was Oz. She had a line that went, "I am Oz, the great and powerful." I laughed because she was so serious when she said it, and she looked anything but powerful. But here she was earnestly delivering her line.

Alfred: My mom never told me she played Oz. I am in a play called *Popposites,* but I don't want to discuss that now. I'd rather ask you questions. So, what was my mom like as a child?

Grandma: She was very serious and responsible. I never had to ask her to do her homework. I never worried that she'd get into trouble. I only worried that she didn't have many friends or much fun.

Alfred: Those are the same ways that I worry my mom.

Grandma: Well, do you have any fun?

Alfred: Now I do — so much that I sometimes get tired and need a break. I have chess club, I am rehearsing for *Popposites,* I am learning about dogs, and I have a lot of friends. Some of them need help with their homework, especially math, and I always say "yes."

Grandma: Why, Alfred, that is wonderful. I'm so glad to hear that.

Alfred: It's because of my mom. She wanted me to have more friends, so she brought in Coach, who I didn't want but am now happy about.

Grandma: She sounds like a much better mom than me.

Alfred: I wouldn't say that. I think you know that I like numbers. I like to rate things on a scale of one to ten, low to high. So, my mom is a ten, which I only realized this year. I don't know enough to rate you, and anyways I wouldn't, but I am sure she learned a lot from you. I can just tell where she gets her smarts from—which also means where I get my smarts from.

Grandma: Alfred, you are a flatterer.

Alfred: Not really. Sometimes, I am too honest, but I only realize it afterward. And then I feel bad. I have another question. When you were angry after Grandpa died, how did that anger show up?

Grandma: It showed up in funny places. I stopped caring about how I looked. I didn't talk too much—just what I needed to say. I didn't give much attention to your mom, which I felt bad about, but I couldn't do anything different. Then one day, I was invited to play the card game called "bridge." Some women in the neighborhood felt bad for me. And that was the beginning of me slowly getting out of my shell. You see, I needed some friends too.

Alfred: Were you less angry afterward?

Grandma: Yes. I did things like occasionally bake cookies for your mom. I got involved in the church. But I didn't really help make your mom's world bigger. I wish I had.

Alfred: Grandma, my mom is happy now. I wouldn't feel too bad. Last question. Did you ever think about getting married again?

Grandma: No. I'd been down that road, and it was hard. Have you ever heard the saying, "It's not how many times you get knocked down? It's how many times you get back up?" I think I couldn't stand the idea of getting knocked down again. I wasn't sure that I'd get back up.

Alfred: I have never heard that saying before. That's a good one. I might even use it sometime. Grandma, thank you for talking to me about things that could easily make you sad — all over again.

Grandma: Yes, they could, but then I am talking to you, and that changes the whole experience. In you, I see hope.

Alfred: Grandma, how about you come and watch some Naruto with me? I can explain it, we can have some globs, and you can even ask me a few questions.

Grandma: Sure. But I have one request. When you talk to Coach, ask him about resilience which is something I don't expect you to understand. Find out what it is and why it's important. It will be helpful in these types of conversations.

Alfred: Ok, Grandma. In Coach's words, "You just gave me an assignment." I didn't need a seventh-inning stretch anyway. Coach told me to relax and instead, I chose to use my time to talk to you. It was so interesting, that I am going to bet there is a part two in our future. Ok?

Grandma: Not a problem. Especially if we get to end with eating your favorite cookies.

Chunk 32:

Back in Coach's Saddle

*A*fter Alfred's chat with Grandma, he is back with Coach. He can't wait to tell Coach what he learned. He wonders where they go next.

Coach: Hello Alfred! You look rested—dare I say content?

Alfred: Well, I've been walking Calvin, which really does make me happy. I understand why there are so many dogs and dog lovers in the world. You think dogs are just slobbery, smelly creatures who like to lick you, but the more you understand them, you realize there is a lot going on in that brain of theirs. And there is no end to the love they give you. It's great!

Coach: So it seems I can assume that Calvin and Alfred are becoming good friends. Let me guess—you had part two of a conversation with your mom on puppies.

Alfred: Nope. I'm giving her some time because I know the probability of "yes" will be higher — by probably 20 to 30 percent. It's all about playing the odds.

Coach: So, is there anything else you want to discuss, or should I pick the topic?

Alfred: I talked with my grandma and learned a few things. It turns out she loves numbers too. She was a bookkeeper, which helped her keep, "A roof over our heads and food on the table" — those were her exact words.

Coach: Interesting. Maybe, your love of numbers comes from her.

Alfred: That's exactly what I said. Afterward, I introduced her to Naruto, and we ate globs. We agreed to do this again. She also said some other stuff, but I want to change topics.

Coach: Ok — to what?

Alfred: *Popposites* and Hannah. I thought *Popposites* was going well, but as we get near showtime, people are stressed out. And Hannah isn't helping. She's irritable too. As the culture builder, I first decided to name our current mood so that we could fix it. I've called it "snappy" because everyone snaps at each other. It's not fun.

Coach: So, you're back in the culture-building business?

Alfred: Exactly. I thought I was done.

Coach: My advice? You're never done when it comes to building a healthy culture.

Alfred: Well, this can't be my job for life. Anyway, I went back to the old trick of using humor, only this time I suggested pet humor. Do you know which dog keeps the best time?

Coach: A clock-er spaniel?

Alfred: That's a great answer, but no. The answer is a watchdog. There were some other good ones too. Mitchell offered a horse joke. Why did the pony have to gargle?

Coach: Why?

Alfred: Because it was a little horse. We had fun, and we even got Hannah to laugh.

Coach: It sounds like you were very helpful.

Alfred: Well, we'd done it once before, so as the saying goes—I know how you and my mom both like sayings—"history was on my side." Also, choosing pet humor is a winner because pets love us no matter what. Maybe the same will be true about the *Popposites'* audience.

Coach: So you subliminally planted a theme of love and appreciation.

Alfred: "Subliminally" is a big word that fortunately for you I know, and it's also bigger than me. You are giving me more than I deserve. Anyway, the real question is whether I can help Hannah.

Coach: Ask her.

Alfred: What? Why is she so unhappy?

Coach: Or whether you can be of help.

Alfred: That could feel awkward. She might not know.

Coach: Or she might. Don't assume. Otherwise, you risk being a know-betterer.

Alfred: But that's something I'm good at.

Coach: You're not as good as you once were. Besides, what do you lose by asking?

Alfred: She might feel more uncomfortable. I can tell from her eyes that she doesn't like making contact like she used to. I pay attention to the eyes these days. Calvin taught me that.

Coach: I have one more thing to offer before you to talk to Hannah. Notice that I assume you will. Hannah's behavior might be a result of what I call "When your anger doesn't know its home." Hannah is preparing to leave, and she probably has a lot of feelings rumbling around inside her. Maybe she thinks about her friends or her mom. Things she will miss. She might be angry and doesn't know where to put those emotions.

Alfred: She also has a lot to be happy about. She'll get to see her dad. She'll probably do much less brother-sitting. Maybe they'll even do something fun like going to a water park.

Coach: Well, you can bring that up when you speak with her.

Alfred: I wish I knew the probability that she would like this type of conversation or even the probability that I could be helpful.

Coach: This is one of those moments where data doesn't help.

Alfred: Ok, but so you know, this is not comfortable for me. It's what I call the "soft squishy bucket of emotions." You'd be better at speaking with Hannah.

Coach: But she has a friendship with you. Don't be scared. You've got this.

Alfred: That's so funny that you said, "You've got this," because Hannah always says that when she wants to encourage us. She hasn't said it much lately. Maybe she hasn't "got this."

Coach: So, will you speak with Hannah?

Alfred: Well, it sounds like it's going to be this week's assignment. I might need a walk with Calvin afterward.

Coach: When you're talking to Hannah, consider the possibility that sometimes our anger doesn't know it's home.

Alfred: Ok. Can we end today on a funny note? Sort of like our own little culture-building activity? You go first.

Coach: Sure. Here goes. Knock, knock. Who's there? Broken pencil. Broken pencil, who? Never mind. It's pointless.

Alfred: I have a short one you might like. Do you know where

Waldo is? Answer: I think he's trying to find himself. By the way, I think that joke fits us well.

Coach: Yes it does, and on that, it's a wrap. See you next week.

Coach checks in with Alfred's mom. "Today's talk was like no other."

"How so?"

"Well, to use one of your favorite words, we showed range. Grandma, culture building, Hannah's growing irritability, Calvin and puppies, and then what Alfred calls 'the soft squishy basket of emotions.'"

"I've heard Alfred use that expression before. Did he come up with it himself?"

"Yes, he did, and when I suggested that Alfred could help Hannah, he said he wasn't so good with the soft, squishy basket of emotions. Of course, I contested his point, and I think he heard me. But I do like his expression, and I might even use it."

"Yes, I like it too. It sounds like him—smart and simple, and about something he wouldn't necessarily like."

"I noticed that you've skipped over the mention of puppies."

"Well, it seems to be only going in one direction. It would help me if my emotions were softer and squishier there."

Chunk 32: Back in Coach's Saddle

Coach smiles. "If I can be of help, you'll let me know?"

"Sure. I think, though, what I need is some self-talk that starts with, 'Welcome to my new reality.' It's kind of hard to imagine me not welcoming a puppy in our future. Let's leave it there for now. See you next week."

Chunk 33:

Straight Talk and Discovery

*C*oach left Alfred with the toughest assignment yet: Discover why Hannah seems irritable. Alfred considered asking, "What's bugging you" but decided that the odds of a meaningful answer were slim, so he opted for a different approach.

Alfred: Yay, Hannah! We finally get to take a walk. We never do that. We're always so busy—homework, chess club, *Popposites*.

Hannah: Yep. That's us. I had to think about whether I had time for a walk, but then you've been so helpful with *Popposites*, I couldn't say no.

Alfred: Does this mean our walk is more about returning a favor than doing something fun?

Hannah: It's both. I can't lie, Alfred.

Alfred: Well, I'm glad you can't lie, but I'm sad that it's not pure fun.

Hannah: Don't feel bad. Sometimes life is about returning favors. You agreed to be my narrator and culture builder, which turned out to be a big job. I fill in at chess club when you need me. I'm also happy to take a walk, so think of it as an "and" situation.

Alfred: Meaning?

Hannah: That thanking you *and* enjoying the walk are not mutually exclusive. You know what I mean by that, right?

Alfred: Yes, and that is a great use of the word "and" which you delivered with emphasis. I've never used "and" that way before—at least that I know of. It is one of the reasons why I like you so much, Hannah. I learn from you, *and* you always seem to be able to take our conversation up a level. Ya' see how I just used the word "and?" I'm a quick learner.

Hannah: Yes, you are, which is also one of the reasons why I like you so much.

Alfred: Anyway, I've been having a lot of one-on-one conversations lately, and I think I'm getting better at them. I always find out something interesting—and the biggest surprise is that it seldom involves numbers. For example, do you have a favorite color?

Hannah: Well, yes, but why do you ask?

Alfred: Because the answer can sometimes give us clues. My mom loves blue and green because it translates to optimism and growth. I could tell you more, but I'd rather hear about your favorite color.

Hannah: I like red.

Alfred: Do you know why you like red?

Hannah: I've never thought about it. It's just what I'm attracted to. Do you know why I like red?

Alfred: Well, I could come up with some hypotheses. You are my boldest friend, so I think red suits you. You are comfortable being noticed. You don't hide from the spotlight.

Hannah: I never thought about that. Ok. So, what's your favorite color?

Alfred: Maybe brown or yellow, but I don't have a dedicated color. It also might be another case of "and" as in both colors suit me. Brown reminds me of chocolate, which takes me to Soho Globs. Yellow reminds me of Naruto because that's his hair color.

Hannah: So, for you, color relates to things that make you happy.

Alfred: Correct. Speaking of which, what are some things that make you happy?

Hannah: Honestly, not much these days. By the way, this feels more like an interview than just a conversation between friends.

Alfred: Sorry about that.

Hannah: That's ok. I'll consider this as just another part of how I thank you by agreeing to be interviewed. So, what makes me happy? Solving math problems. Saying, "Checkmate." Writing. Spending time with close friends. You.

Alfred: You didn't mention *Popposites.*

Hannah: "*Popposites*" makes me nervous. Maybe "happy" will come. What makes you happy?

Alfred: These days, Joey's dog Calvin makes me happy. He loves to fetch. I should back up. Do you know what "fetch" means? I didn't until Calvin came into my life.

Hannah: Yes, Alfred, I know what it means for dogs to fetch.

Alfred: Well, I never thought about dogs, and now it's what I think about most. They're a puzzle in a different way. They don't use words, but they still express themselves—pretty clearly, too—if you're "dog-smart."

Hannah: Then it sounds like Calvin shares the top spot with baseball statistics as something you enjoy thinking about.

Alfred: I know. Kind of surprising. I've got another question for you: What makes you sad?

Hannah: That one is easy. The thought of leaving my friends this summer. Actually, if it's only for the summer, I'm ok. If my parents decide it's permanent, I won't be.

Alfred: My mom always says, "Let's cross that bridge when we come to it." While I often don't get her sayings—and there are many—I think it applies here. There is no need to worry yet. Do you want to know what makes me sad?

Hannah: Sure.

Alfred: The thought that my mom might say "no" to getting a dog.

Hannah: Can we apply your mom's saying again? Don't be sad unless she says "no." We're not crossing the bridge yet.

Alfred: I think you're misusing the saying, but I get what you mean. I misuse her sayings all the time. So one more question, and then we can just talk like friends. When you are sad, what helps you?

Hannah: I wish I knew. It's not Soho Globs, and I like dogs, but it's not Calvin or dogs in general. I think the act of creating makes me happy. That's why I wrote *Popposites.* Just talking doesn't work. It often makes me more upset.

Alfred: I wonder what Coach would say.

Hannah: Well, get creative. Think, think, think. You've certainly been talking to Coach long enough to guess his response.

Alfred: I think he'd say something about needing to really figure out why you feel sad. I am seeing two possibilities. It would either be "Face your fears" or else "When your anger doesn't know it's home."

Hannah: I get "Face your fears," but the anger one is lost on me.

Alfred: I had that same reaction. Coach is saying that we sometimes place our emotions in funny areas. Like if you are mad about leaving for the summer, and then something small happens at a *Popposites* rehearsal, and you get all upset, the question would be why. Was it what happened at *Popposites*, or is your anger leaking out somewhere else? I think that's what he means.

Hannah: The example you gave feels a little too real. It probably happened, but please don't tell me if it did. I'm not sure I could handle it. Can you ask Coach if the "anger not knowing its home" thing is my problem?

Alfred: Every time I have a one-on-one conversation, I always end up with an assignment for when I talk to Coach. Granny had one too. Now, you. I can ask, but I'm pretty sure he would want to talk to you directly.

Hannah: Maybe at some point, we can make that happen.

Alfred: We can try. Coach is very helpful. Last week I was sad that you were so "snappy"—my term. He told me to talk to you and not to worry. Our friendship would be fine. And it will.

Hannah: Look at you—quant jock, *Popposites* narrator, chess club president, and now I'll call you mini-Coach. You're like our favorite baseball player, Mike Trout. I've got the name right, right? Can I now say that you've got range?

Alfred: Yes, the name is Mike Trout, and I am working on developing range as a person. We know I can't develop range as an athlete. I am not athletic and never will be. By the way, I really like that you said "our" favorite baseball player. I am pretty sure baseball is not your thing, and you said it for me.

Hannah: I might have said it for you, or maybe you've inspired me to love baseball. Either way, though, Coach was right. Our friendship will be fine no matter what happens in terms of where my parents decide that Ben and I will live. The thing is—and you know this about me—I am persuasive, so I think the odds are in our favor that the move is only for the summer.

Alfred: I like that, and I won't ask you for the actual odds. But just talking right now, you seem happier—like your mood has lifted.

Hannah: Yes, you are right, *and* I thank you. See how I just used "and" again? And now I have to head back. See you at rehearsal in a bit.

Alfred: Ok, and once again you brought something interesting to my attention. I might never look at the word "and" in the same way.

Chunk 34:

Blue Sky Abounds

*A*lfred met with Hannah and now has a conversation to report to Coach. Alfred's mood is decidedly upbeat since their last meeting. Coach holds out hope that things are trending well for Alfred, Hannah's good friend and *Popposites* culture builder.

Alfred: What a week! *Popposites*. Hannah. A conversation with my mom. There's so much to catch up on, and I think I only have one question for you.

Coach: Where do you want to start?

Alfred: With *Popposites*. We finally had our show, and it was full of surprises.

Coach: Like what?

Alfred: For starters, Shamisu has a dance number with a guy named Mortie. I've never mentioned Mortie. Right before the show, Hannah gets a call that Mortie can't make it. He's sick. Now we have a big hole to fill. Hannah says, "Alfred, this is your chance to step up—pun intended." I was irritated. "What do you mean 'step up?' I've been stepping up the whole time—narrator, culture builder, memorizing people's lines."

Coach: All true. You've been their MVP.

Alfred: I wouldn't go that far, but Hannah knew she was playing me and started to laugh. She said that she had no right to ask any more of me but that it could be a chance for me to dance with Shamisu. "Hannah," I said, "I don't dance, AND YOU KNOW THAT!"

Coach: So, you stood your ground! Good for you.

Alfred: Well, not exactly. She reminded me that I'd said to the cast, "Our mistakes are a laugh that we didn't plan for." Then she added, "Alfred, this could be the laugh you didn't plan for."

Coach: That Hannah! She is a clever one—how she uses your exact words to get her desired result!

Alfred: Next thing I knew, I was asking Shamisu if I could be behind her on stage, trying to copy her steps. I would look awkward, but maybe I could get a few of the steps down by watching her, and anyway, we could turn a disaster into a comedy.

Coach: Quick thinking, and very generous of you too.

Alfred: Actually, it was desperate thinking and the power of

Hannah. She can pretty much get anyone to do anything. She'd make a great president!

Coach: Well, you never know where she'll end up, but she's a fun one to track.

Alfred: Anyways, we went with my idea, which was just another example of *Popposites*—Shamisu's great dancing alongside my clumsy steps. It went great. People laughed. Hannah was happy. I wasn't embarrassed, though I'm not sure why. And Shamisu was a good sport, who looked even better with her dance moves when compared to me.

Coach: That's a great story.

Alfred: I'm not done. At one moment, the theatre went black. Joey had to work hard to diagnose the problem. Something shorted, and then Joey became our hero and fixed it. The whole night, *Popposites* became a story of "Expect the unexpected."

Coach: It sounds like you coped well.

Alfred: We didn't have too many choices. I kept hearing people say, "We have another laugh we didn't plan for." Then at the end, we gave Hannah a bouquet. She deserved flowers and more if you ask me. Then the cast surprised me with a present— *Puppies for Dummies*—the best book ever! I guess my secret of wanting a puppy was out. I was super psyched to be appreciated and to have a book that I can't wait to read.

Coach: Your mom must have been so proud.

Alfred: Yes, I think so. I gave her the book with a smile. Talk about hearing unspoken words. Hers were so loud!

Coach: Yes, she was probably saying, "It always comes back to dogs, doesn't it?"

Alfred: And also, "How did we get to this place?" which I can't answer. Things happen, and as you've taught me, we need to keep an open mind. I know that her mind is opening because she has started asking lots of dog questions. Things like, "How long do you think a puppy be left alone?" and "Who will train the puppy?" I just listen and then answer as best I can.

Coach: So, you also mentioned you talked with Hannah?

Alfred: Yes, we took a walk before the *Popposites'* show. I was nervous, but I used my curiosity to help me, and I was careful not to be a know-betterer. I asked her what her favorite color was, which turns out to be red.

Coach: Was she curious as to why?

Alfred: Definitely, but she figures things out quickly. I also asked her what makes her happy, and she said, "Not much lately." That led to a conversation about moving to a small town in Indiana— Terre Haute she said—to be with her dad, and she will miss her friends. She hopes it's only for the summer.

Coach: Nice that you got her to open up.

Alfred: Well, then I got stuck. She asked me what Coach would say after I mentioned that sometimes she can get really mad about small things. I think I called her reaction "at times disproportionate," which made me sound older than I am, but at least not a know-betterer. Anyway, I think I often sound old for my age. You can thank my mom for that. I don't worry about it with Hannah, though, because her vocabulary is bigger than mine.

Coach: So what did you say to Hannah when she asked for my take? It makes me feel like my words really are important.

Alfred: I think you know that your words matter, and I kind of guessed at what I thought you'd say. I offered Hannah either "Face your fears" or "When your anger doesn't know it's home." She asked me to ask you which one it was—if it even was. I also had to explain the "your anger" saying, which I think I did right.

Coach: I feel honored and respected, and mostly, I am touched that you could do this for Hannah. At such an early age, you're becoming quite the coach.

Alfred: Not really, but Hannah is waiting for your answer.

Coach: Alfred, you know this more than anyone: answers don't come that easily. She will need to work for it.

Alfred: I told her that, and I also said that I'd ask you.

Coach: So, you said you had a question?

Alfred: It's about good news, bad news. The good news is that Hannah is back to being a friend I enjoy hanging out with. The bad news is that she leaves in a month and might not be coming back. I'm very sad.

Coach: That's real and a testament to your friendship. When I have those kinds of feelings, I work on accepting them. I try to not deny my sadness, and I try to identify some joy. Take my mom, for example. She isn't doing great. She and I both know that. But then I remind myself how lucky I've been to have her as my mom, and she still can pepper me with questions and interesting thoughts at the ripe age of 89!

Alfred: This sounds like your "glass half-full" lesson. By the way, I think I am lucky with the mom I got, too—especially if she ends up saying "yes" to a puppy.

Coach: I think we just figured out this week's assignment. When you are feeling sad, what do you tell yourself to stay positive and hopeful? You might not have an answer, but all I ask is to give it some thought.

Alfred: Ok.

Coach: And Alfred—really nice work you did.

Coach checks in on Alfred's mom. "I don't know where to start, so I think I won't."

"Coach, that doesn't sound like you. You always have something to say."

Chunk 34: Blue Sky Abounds

With a very soft voice, Coach smiles and admits, "Eleanor, I think Alfred is well on his way to being Coach number two. How he spoke with Hannah and how he volunteered himself in the act of comedy—well, there are no words."

Alfred's mom, visibly moved, replies, "Thank god for those unspoken words. Can you hear my silent gratitude?"

And with those words, Coach heads out with a wink of the eye. "Next week, then."

Chunk 35:

Coach and Hannah Explore Being Happy

Alfred did as Hannah has asked and inquired whether Coach would speak with her. "Hannah has a lot on her mind," Alfred said, "and a little of you would go a long way." Coach was reluctant at first but since he asked Alfred to be there for Hannah, he felt compelled to lead by example, and he explained this all to Alfred. "We can't ask others to do what we don't do ourselves, only in my case this is slightly more complicated. I need permission from Hannah's parent to speak with Hannah."

Alfred did two things as a result. He asked Hannah to have his mom call Coach and grant approval for a session. Alfred also suggested that Hannah write a brief note to Coach to explain why she needed to meet. "He knows very little about you, so think of it like *Popposites*, and set the stage," Alfred suggested.

After Coach and Hannah's mom spoke, Hannah explained in a note that she wanted to be happier and was hoping that Coach could help "unlock the mystery" about why she felt down.

Hannah and Coach finally meet as the school year draws near to a close.

Hannah: Coach—can I call you "Coach?"

Coach: Absolutely

Hannah: Coach, thank you for agreeing to meet with me. I have lots of questions. So how does this work?

Coach: How does what work?

Hannah: How do we start? Do I just start talking, and then you say something when you've figured something out? Do you ask me questions first? I can do whatever works.

Coach: Hannah, there is no "one way." Why don't we start with you telling me why you wanted to meet. I read your note, which was helpful, but I'd like to understand more.

Hannah: Sure. I'm not happy. I usually am. So, I want to fix it. I want your help.

Coach: Ok. That is very succinct. Why aren't you happy?

Hannah: That's where I need help. I think it starts with my having to spend the summer with my dad and brother—two hours away from here. There will be no friends around. It's also possible that my unhappiness started earlier when my mom had to increase her hours at work, leaving me to do more brother-sitting.

Coach: Well, you already seem to have a pretty good handle on at least some of the reasons why you're unhappy.

Hannah: Yes, but in the words of Alfred, which might actually just be your words, my unhappiness sometimes leaks into areas that aren't really related. I don't think that's good. He said that my anger doesn't know it's home. So, we need to fix that.

Coach: Hmm. Are you aware when you are having your anger "leak out" to borrow your phrase?

Hannah: You mean Alfred's phrase. Maybe sometimes, but not always. I am just lucky that I have good friends who love me even when I misbehave.

Coach: I wouldn't call it "misbehave." That's being too hard on you. I would say you are finding an outlet for your emotions.

Hannah: Fine. That makes sense. So, if we go with that, and I think we should, what can we do?

Coach: Hannah, I've got a question. Are you used to solving problems right away?

Hannah: Definitely. What do we get by waiting?

Coach: Well, sometimes it takes a while to solve a problem. There can be a series of steps required to figure things out. The clock can't always be our master.

Hannah: I was afraid you were going to say something like that.

Coach: I'm just being honest. If I were you, I'd want to know what makes me angry? I might want to go back over the last year and see what things happened that I didn't like. I might want to see if I had a chance to voice my feelings. I might want to know if I felt heard and whether I was able to do anything that could alter whatever it was that I didn't like.

Hannah: That is a lot of figuring out. For me to do that, I would need some patience. Patience is not something I am good at.

Coach: Just because you're not good at it today doesn't mean you won't be good at it tomorrow—or eventually. Aren't we always trying to grow and build new skills? Maybe you can put patience on your to-do list. You seem like someone who has many lists.

Hannah: Wow, it didn't take you long to figure me out. Now I know why Alfred likes you so much. You are really smart at reading people. Of course, I use lists. Otherwise, I couldn't do as many things as I do—and hopefully, do them well.

Coach: Well, this is only a start, and soon you'll be headed out, but maybe make a list of things that upset you when you suddenly feel irritated. It might help you begin to understand the nature of your anger. It gives us a helpful place to start.

Hannah: So that's my assignment? I know Alfred always has an assignment.

Coach: Put it this way. Were we to continue to meet, this is where I would want to start. Then we could know whether it's fear, or anger, or maybe too much on your plate, or the high expectations you place on yourself, or a mix of everything that contributes to an unhappy mood.

Hannah: Alfred did not exaggerate. You really are helpful. I am hoping to come back with a list—a chronology, really—of what has made me upset. If I do, then will you make time for me? Every week like you did with Alfred? We are very different people, but I am pretty sure you would learn to like me and would want to help me just like you have Alfred.

Coach: Oh, of that, I am sure.

Hannah: And we have our appreciation of Alfred in common, which is a great place to start.

Coach: Yes. Let's take it one step at a time. You're heading out. The school year is coming to a close. Let's leave it that you will begin to chronicle moments that bother you. Since you like to write, this should be right up your alley.

Hannah: Sounds good. And there is one more thing you should know about me.

Coach: Yes?

Hannah: My mom says that I like to be in the driver's seat, which is funny because that's where she always puts me—taking care of everything. So, I am going to try very hard to drive myself back to town at the end of the summer. I mean that figuratively because I am too young to actually drive. But I fully intend to be back!

Coach: I think your mom has a good understanding of you. The image of you being in the driver's seat fits. If, or maybe I should say, "when," you come back, I look forward to seeing your list. And remember, the clock can't always be your master.

Hannah: I like the sound of that… "The clock can't always be my master." Hopefully, at some point, I will actually understand those words. Thank you, Coach. We will be in touch. I just know it.

Chunk 36:

Change is in the Air

*C*hange is in the air. Alfred is fretting about Hannah's departure. There are other things lingering on his mind, but he can't quite put words to it—"yet"—he tells himself. "Once your goal is understanding your world, it is hard to control where your mind goes," he says in epic self-talk. "Playing a good game of chess is so much easier."

No matter. There are two more weeks of school, and then a quiet or not-yet-defined summer awaits. Uncertainty is all around, but Alfred tries to steady himself by considering the glass half full. "It's the first summer ever when I feel sad at saying goodbye to friends at the end of the school year. It feels like a *Popposite* moment—good and bad at the same time," he tells himself.

In the meantime, Alfred's mom is considering his request for a puppy.

Coach: Hey Alfred! How are you doing today?

Alfred: Not sure, to be honest.

Coach: That's a change. I'm used to hearing a very positive response. So, what's up?

Alfred: Well, we're at the end of the school year. Hannah is heading out. My mom hasn't decided about a puppy. My mind is going everywhere. In short, change is all around, and I'm not sure I like it.

Coach: I think you mean, "Change is all around, and I don't like it." Most of us don't.

Alfred: This sounds like the one time where I might be like the majority.

Coach: It will probably help if you look at your feelings through a different lens. Maybe you're sad because of how good the year has been, and you don't want to let it go. You've built some great friendships. You've taken generosity to a new level as the narrator in *Popposites*. We both know how much you didn't want to do that role — or any role for that matter — but you wanted to help Hannah. You've also discovered why people love dogs.

Alfred: And don't forget that I view numbers differently. They're still really important to me, but I know that soft squishy things matter too. And I had some hard conversations with Grandma, my mom, and Hannah. And those conversations have just created more questions for me. So, I just know that I have changed some, and I'm not even done. Trust me. I've still got some unasked questions in me.

Coach: Well, we're never done—kind of like being a culture builder, as you recall—but even still, you've got a big list of things to be proud of.

Alfred: Thank you. Still, it doesn't change my mood. I feel sad, not proud.

Coach: Totally understandable.

Alfred: Since I consider you to be the master of all things practical, do you have any advice for how I can manage my mood? My mom says that I'm a little "blue"—that's what she calls it—and says it's because transitions are hard. She says that I'm transitioning to an "ill-defined summer" to use her words. On a scale of one to ten, my mood is a two or three. I'd like it to be at least a five or six. Any suggestions?

Coach: Your mom is right that transitions are hard. We don't like uncertainty, and we don't like endings.

Alfred: And also, my mind is rumbling around a lot. I am starting to wonder about things that I've never really asked about— like a missing dad, for example—maybe because I am thinking of things I will miss like Hannah or have missed for reasons I don't really know. Any idea what should I do?

Coach: Have patience and faith. Faith that, over time, answers will come, and you will figure things out. My shortest and simplest advice to you Alfred—bet on yourself.

Alfred sits quietly, looking down, then looking up towards the ceiling, and then finally meets Coach's eye.

Alfred: Ok, but that's kind of vague, especially since anytime I place a bet, I always consider the odds first, and here, there are no odds.

Coach: Oh, Alfred. You make me laugh. I am going through my own difficult transition, so we're in the same place in some ways. Uncertainty is hard.

Alfred: Well, I like talking about you more, and besides, you've now got me curious. I know I should respect your privacy, but how are we alike right now? And feel free to leave me wondering if it's too uncomfortable to talk about.

Coach: I'm not holding back on you now. My mom is having a rough time. I think we're near the end of the line.

Alfred: Oh wow! What will you do? And do you have someone to talk to? It's very helpful, you know. You can't always be Coach. You also might need a coach of your own.

Coach: I will go be with her. That's what I want to do.

Alfred: Until the very end?

Coach: Yes.

Alfred: When will you go?

Coach: As soon as I can finish up here.

Alfred: I think you know that you're not finished with me. Especially because I have some unanswered questions that will probably require more help on your part.

Coach: Alfred, it is my privilege to continue to help you, even if I'm not sure you still need me. I will spend time with my mom for the foreseeable future, but then, you've got me.

Alfred: I don't want to sound selfish, but can I see you one more time before you leave? I mean, with you and Hannah both leaving and no puppy in sight, one more meeting would be really helpful.

Coach: We can make that happen.

Alfred: Thank you. It's a wonderful example of your being generous with me. I promise to return the kindness.

Coach: You already have. Remember how you made my mom Soho Globs? She loved them. Your assignment is to make a list of things you want to discuss, and we'll talk next week.

Alfred: That's so funny. Just saying the word "list" reminds me of Hannah. She's a big list-maker. You'll find that out if you continue with her. See you next week.

Coach checks in with Alfred's mom. "Eleanor, I know Alfred is going through a tough time, and it can't be that easy being his mom right now. But I know he'll figure his way through this. He is, after all, a 5-tool player."

At the mere mention of a 5-tool player, Alfred's mom smiles. "Yes, he has range, and I'm not worried about Alfred in the long run, but our short term could be rocky."

"One more thing I need to share," says Coach. "I am going to spend time with my mom. She doesn't have much longer, and I want to be with her."

"Oh, wow. I feel for you. This must be very hard. Does Alfred know?"

"Yes. He asked if we could talk one more time before I head out, and I agreed."

"Well, then, that settles it. No Hannah. No Coach. He will have fallen into that hole and will need some help making his way out. I don't know if I ever shared my favorite episode of *West Wing* that led me to you."

"You did, and I then watched it, and have watched it again since. It is poignant and aspirational. It reminded me of why I do what I do."

Alfred's mom smiled, just to know that she could have that impact on Coach, after the many ways he has touched them. And now her mind was made up.

"Don't tell Alfred, but we are going to get a puppy. It will keep Alfred busy, lift his mood, and earn me some 'mom points.' I'm sure I'll need them at some point."

"I'm not so sure you'll need them, but your timing is perfect. You might just become Alfred's new super hero if you're not already. See you next week."

Chunk 37:

Click Your Heels Three Times

With Coach and Hannah heading out, Alfred fears he will be lonely which he shared with his friend Mitchell. Mitchell reminded him that Alfred is often the grown-up in the room that his friends have come to rely upon, "So I hope you can keep it together."

Alfred hopes so too and thinks it just might be time for another "mom-talk." Alfred knows he needs something. He's just not sure what, so why not ask one of the smartest people in his world?

Alfred: Hey, mom. Are you busy?

Mom: Never too busy for you. What's on your mind?

Alfred: Coach and Hannah are both leaving—at least for the summer.

Mom: And?

Alfred: And I am going to feel lonely. I've worked so hard to get to where I am. How do I know I won't lose it?

Mom: Lose what? Your growth? Your awareness of people and what they bring to us?

Alfred: Yes, and probably more if I really think about it.

Mom: I understand your fear, but I am not worried. Tonight, you and I are going to watch *Wizard of Oz*. Do you know why?

Alfred: I have no idea. I am going to guess that you're finally tired of *Friends*. Finally! Thank God.

Mom: No on two counts. I'm not tired of *Friends,* and that's not why we're going to watch *Wizard of Oz*. It's because of what Dorothy comes to understand at the end. It is very relevant to you right now.

Alfred: The only thing I remember about Dorothy is that she had a dog named "Toto"—a terrier if I remember correctly. Well, it's not the only thing I remember about Dorothy, but it is the most important.

Mom: Wow, look at you. "A terrier." You have progressed in your dog knowledge to actually know the breeds. How very Alfred of you.

Alfred: And by that, I think you mean a compliment.

Mom: Of course. But getting back to Dorothy, she wanted to go back to Kansas, and Glinda, the good witch, tells her to click her heels three times.

Alfred: I do remember that — still not sure why that relates to me.

Mom: Because Dorothy could have clicked her heels the whole time and returned to Kansas, but she didn't know she had the power to do so. Glinda never told her, and do you know why?

Alfred: No, but to be fair, I'm much better with numbers than understanding movies or literature in general. I truly have no clue why Glinda kept Dorothy in the dark, but I do wonder why Glinda settled on the number "three."

Mom: Let's not focus on the number right now. The reason Glinda didn't come to her rescue was that, as Glinda explains, Dorothy has to discover her power for herself. I think the same is true for you. What you've discovered this year has been there all along, but you had to see it with your own eyes to believe it. And that is why I am not worried. You know something now that you didn't know before.

Alfred: And maybe Toto helped too. Just saying — it could be multifactorial.

Mom: Alfred, you make me laugh, and I'm about to make you very happy. This is the summer that we introduce a puppy into our family. Before you get all happy, there will be some rules I am going to set down.

Alfred: I am good with rules, and thank you for making my day—actually my summer—actually my life!

Mom: So, we will need to figure out what breed and then discuss how we train this new puppy. Alfred, we must commit to training. It will be work—hard work—but you've got a whole summer to start the process. And to do some grown-up speak for a minute, our investment will pay dividends. That means training will be especially worthwhile.

Alfred: I promise you I will be responsible. Wow, this day is feeling like *Popposites* all over again. I started off so sad, and I am ending up happy. I need to tell Joey. We need to figure out where we get our puppy. There is so much to be done. Mom, I gotta go. Thank you, thank you.

Mom: Wait, before you leave, if we get a female puppy, I like the name "Nellie." The reasons aren't that interesting, but I am going to ask you to consider my request.

Alfred: Done.

Mom: Also, I want you to channel Glinda's lesson for Dorothy. You've always had the power in you, but now you know it.

Alfred: Mom, there is only one way to end this conversation. You are my Glinda. I want to go catch Joey now. Love you.

Mom: One more thing I wanted to mention. Grandma is coming for a visit. Evidently, she so enjoyed her last visit with that she is now going to make it monthly! Imagine that.

Alfred: Ok. That's great, I think. I do have more things I want to discuss with her. Do you know if she likes walking dogs? That would be great for me, for Grandma, and for the new puppy, and by the way, "Nellie" is fine.

Chunk 38:
The Big Reveal or
The Question I Never Asked Until I Did

I am becoming more like Hannah and maybe even Coach. Now when my world feels like it has been turned upside down, I write down my feelings because words work well when numbers don't.

I was so excited that Grandma was coming and that there would be more of her in my life. She brings conversation, news, energy, and openness—all of which I like. Also, because I have a lot of unanswered questions that swirl in my head, Grandma can be helpful.

When Joey and I were talking the other day, he asked me if I knew who my dad was. It got me thinking about something that I had shut out—on purpose. It was the easiest thing to do, and I think it also helped my mom. But here was Grandma, and Joey's question was fresh, so I thought maybe this would be the time to learn more.

And I did. Our conversation sent a shock through me, and I wasn't sure what to do. Coach was leaving soon. My mom needed a break. I decided that the best thing would be for me to sit down and process my new reality—as if I were going to write an essay for my Language Arts class. I took care to make each word matter. I tried to think both big (like what does knowing something about my dad mean to me) and small (like will I ever forget how my mom cried in the kitchen).

There was a lot to digest, and here is what I wrote.

The Big Reveal
By Alfred

The moment was very awkward and boy, do I know awkward. I had often wondered who my dad was, but I also had the feeling that I should never bring it up. That was ok because there was so much else that needed my attention. I was focusing on people outside my family—my "friends in the making" is how I referred to it. Inside my family, there was Grandma, my mom, and now Coach.

Coach isn't a blood relative, but he's like one. It counts that he roots for me and gives me advice in a way that I can hear it. He's on my side. Outside my family, though, there were a lot of kids that I was trying to get to know. "Know" means more than their name—which is how it starts for me with a scribble on my hand. And that's *name* only—no room for a preferred personal pronoun.

On this one life-changing afternoon, I had a chat with Grandma. I can ask her anything. That's how we are together. Little did I know that our conversation would be a turning point in how I viewed me, the world, and my mom (of course). That maybe sounds melodramatic, but it's true. I went straight to the topic of Grandpa because my mom had told me of their roller-coaster marriage. They had separated at a time when people didn't do that type of thing. As I was to learn, they later realized that they still loved each other and were about to give it another go.

Unfortunately, Grandpa died of a heart attack before they actually had their second chance. Grandma found a small silver lining. She's like that—always finding something positive to say. She told me that while it was still painful to think about never having had round two of their marriage, "At least we rediscovered our love." Then she let out a big sigh. Her sigh sounded to me like a scab that would never really heal.

It was at that point that Grandma introduced me to what she refers to as "my favorite word in the whole English dictionary that you, my dear Alfred, need to 'internalize.'" The literal part of me, which is most of me, didn't know what to make of "internalize." We don't eat words, and where are they to live if they are inside us? So, I substituted "internalize" for "really understand." I hope I got it right.

Grandma continued, "Whatever you do in life, it will not go as planned. There will be setbacks. Ask your mom." As I was sitting there, hanging on her every word, still guessing Grandma's favorite word (contenders included peaceful, insightful, curious, and loyal), I got stuck thinking about my mom having had some "setbacks." What were they, and why didn't I know about them?

Then Grandma revealed her favorite word, and in such a firm and precise way that I can still hear it: "Re-sil-i-ence." She made sure I heard every syllable. I kind of knew the meaning of the word, but my face said otherwise because she then added, "Think of it as bouncing back, or to put it in your terms, staging a ninth-inning rally in a game you seemed sure to lose."

Grandma suggested that I discuss "resilience" with Coach because, and I quote, "He needs to make sure that you add that to your 5-piece-toolkit'." Well, she almost got Alfred-speak right, which she said with such a smile and conviction. She added, as if to emphasize her point, "I know you've already picked out your five tools but either make it six or replace one with 're-sil-i-ence.'"

By now, my head was spinning. I had a word that I needed to "internalize," a baseball analogy that I didn't think fit, my five tools up for consideration, and most importantly, a nagging question about my mom's "setbacks," which I took to mean life events that didn't go well.

My head felt dizzy with confusion. I knew that I would need another candid talk with my mom and probably a double session with Coach to work through whatever I was about to learn. A double session would be a first.

I can only imagine the look on my face as I considered all this because I then heard Grandma say that we had talked enough. "Let's go have some Soho Globs as you call them and watch some Naruto. Later, if you still feel as confused as you look right now, I suggest you go talk with your mom."

After we had some globs and watched Naruto (I think Grandma mostly watched me watching Naruto), I agreed that talking to my mom about her "setbacks" was next, but could Grandma give me any pointers so that I was sure to land on the right space? "My mom and I aren't much for long talks," I added to emphasize the need for direction.

Somewhat hesitantly, Grandma offered, "Ask your mom how she picked herself up after David died. I honestly didn't know how she would continue on or where she'd find her strength. But she did."

Wow! Talk about a stunner. I stumbled through the rest of our visit, gave Grandma a hug, and then went straight to my mom.

Until this point, I had looked at my mom as someone very serious and doing her best job—which seemed pretty good—to raise me. I never considered the idea that she had a past or that there was some dark period she had to overcome or, even worse, bury. My cheery Grandma would sometimes say to my mom, "Don't be so glum." I looked up "glum" in the dictionary and decided that Grandma wasn't really being fair. Besides, people are different in how much happy energy they show the world.

Still, after hearing the name "David," I thought there might be a reason for her serious, "glum" mood. Suddenly, I was on a mission to unravel the mystery of my mom's past, find out who David was, and then decide if "resilience" really applied. I knew that immaculate conception did not apply to my mom, so clearly, there had to be somebody in the picture. I was guessing it was David. And so, with Grandma's encouragement, I entered the kitchen with a pit in my stomach—the kind I feel when a sci-fi movie is about to stage the apocalypse. I was scared as heck.

My mom had just finished cleaning up, and we were about to go watch *Friends* and have what my mom calls "our bonding moment." But first, I needed to talk. Here's how it started:

Me: Mom, we need to talk. I did warn you after our first heart-to-heart conversation that there would be more. Our last was fun and happy. You passed along Glinda's lesson to Dorothy and told me we could get a puppy. Now, though, I am back with a more difficult conversation.

Mom: Sometimes, I think my middle name is difficult, so let's have it. What do you want to discuss?

Me: Who was my dad?

There was complete silence, and my mom looked particularly awkward. It's as if she seemed to suddenly shrink. Her shoulders became hunched over as she looked down, and then she took a big breath.

I continued. "Grandma was talking to me about resilience which turns out to be her favorite word in the English dictionary. She said that you had a lot of it, and I should ask you about it. She even mentioned a name that I had never heard of before—David."

More silence. And then slowly, my mom looked up. In a very small voice, my mom said, "Ok. We can talk. Let's sit down, though. I knew this was a conversation we would have sooner or later. The 'sooner' seems to be now."

We didn't get through the entire story, but I did learn a lot. David was the love of my mom's life. They met in college. My mom thought that they would spend the rest of their life together. It sounded like David thought so too. But he was a journalist, and after graduation, he went to go work for a newspaper. Back then, it was "newspapers"—my mom made sure to tell me that.

They would see each other on weekends, and their commitment stayed strong. David eventually moved to D.C. for the job, but even then, they made it work—back and forth, back and forth. Then, two years into the job, he got his big break. He got to cover the unrest in Asia. My mom visited him in D.C. before he headed out because she wasn't sure when he would be back. She said that she still remembers every moment of that weekend. The plan was for David to return back to the Midwest after completing this one big assignment.

David never made it back. One month on the job, David got caught in the line of fire in some Iraqi-Kurdish battle. Shortly after, my mom found out that she was pregnant. When we got to this point in the story, her tears turned into sobs. I didn't know what to do—hug her, give her some space, look down like she was doing, or make eye contact, which Coach has encouraged me to do more of.

My mom explained that she was determined to be strong and, in some weird way, make David proud of how she would continue to live life and raise me. I was, after all, their love child.

This was as far as we could go before I said to my mom, "You don't have to talk anymore. Thank you." And then I hugged her.

I didn't even think about it. It's just what I needed to do—for me. She really had been through a lot, and until this moment, I had no idea of any of it.

I can share this moment now because two weeks have passed and given me some time to think. At first, I was angry. Why did I have to ask to be told? Why did she carry this inside for so long? Wouldn't knowing something about my dad have helped me?

As Coach later explained, anger has many stages. I got to the point where I realized how many ways this discovery could help me. I would now understand my mom better. She was serious, and maybe she was "glum"—to borrow my Grandma's words—for a good reason.

I have always prided myself on my math skills. For whatever reason, I am good with numbers. But now, if genetics holds true, maybe I am good with words too. Maybe I have some writing in me—like Hannah. I am going to test that. If it's true, I will have to figure out which of my five tools would be replaced to make room for writing.

I believe I am on course to go from "anger to gratitude" to borrow Coach's words, and I will eventually see Grandma's big reveal as a gift that I will somehow re-gift to my mom. The new truth will add more "layers" to me—Coach's term—and I am guessing, make me a more worthwhile person to hang out with.

At that moment in the kitchen, though, my mom and I didn't finish our conversation. There is still so much more I want to know, but I am back to reminding myself to be patient. I was left with a funny thought, though. Learning about my dad, who now has a name, felt like a "big reveal"—the kind that couples do when they announce their baby's gender.

From this thought, my mind took me to Hannah and *Popposites*. Maybe there is a sequel called *The Big Reveal* where we encourage our friends to share a surprising story in their life. I need to talk to Hannah. That's why I used "we." Hannah will be a big help to me. She always is.

My last thought in finishing this piece is that my teacher likes to remind us of Aristotle's saying that the total is greater than the sum of the parts. I think this is probably good news because I just found out that I have another part to me. I will need to get to know it though, first.

Chunk 39:

I've Got the Moody Blues

*E*ver since I talked to my mom and found out who my dad was and why he is no longer alive, I can't shake my sadness. I would have liked him somewhere in my life. Instead, he is a memory that I will never get to really know.

I stayed away from the topic of "Who's my dad" for the longest time because something inside me told me not to go there. Coach told me that I was using "my instincts," but that kind of surprised me because I run on numbers, not instincts. At least I did.

On occasion, I try to pay attention to what I call "soft squishy" things, which loosely translates to emotions, but that's still not instincts. Is it possible that I "got em" but don't know? I bet my dad would never have used the half-word "em" because he was a journalist. Journalists use real words.

So, what did I do after my talk with my mom? Well, for the first week, I didn't speak to her too much—except for when it came to logistics. How would I get home from school? When was the chess club meeting? That kind of thing. When we ate dinner, it was very quiet. I answered her questions, but it was more like "yes," "no," and "maybe." Occasionally she'd hear, "I don't know." She knew I was upset, but she didn't push it. Coach said she was doing exactly the right thing—giving me space to process what I learned and work through my anger.

I read about journalists who died in the line of duty. It occurs more than I thought. At least thirty journalists were killed in the field in 2020. So, it happens. One night I started actually "talking" to my mom again—not just answering questions. I asked if David had parents or a brother or sister, and if so, could I meet them? That threw her. She's still thinking about my request.

The day after my mom told me about David, I had a session with Coach. I didn't feel like going, but I wouldn't stand him up. Also, he was heading out soon, so I didn't want to let the opportunity pass. When Coach saw me, he could tell I was not in a mood to talk. I briefly shared what I had learned, and then there was quiet.

The quiet was so long that I started to count in my head, "One Mississippi, two Mississippi…." When I got to thirty, Coach finally spoke. I still remember what he said.

"Alfred, you don't have to talk or even be here if you don't want. I am here for you, but sometimes we really prefer that no one is around us. That might be how you feel right now."

I remember shaking my head as if to indicate, "Yes."

Then Coach followed, "Is there anything I can do for you?"

Now, this intrigued me because if he could make my mood go away, I was all for it. I responded, "How long will I feel this way? My mom calls it 'feeling blue,' and it's not a feeling I'm used to. Coach, if you can get me through this faster, I'd appreciate it."

Coach smiled. Then he offered, "Alfred, everyone heals at a different rate. I know you like numbers, but I can't give you one. I can tell you that how you are processing the information feels healthy. I can also tell you that because you have a great mom and good friends, and you yourself are very special, you will get through this and come out stronger."

There was a pause. Then Coach continued, "It's like a *Popposite* moment as I understand the word. Right now, you feel very low and maybe unsure of yourself, but I predict that before you know it, you will find a new kind of strength that you haven't had before."

When Coach said this, I smiled. It may have been my first real smile in over a week. When my mom made me Soho Globs, I gave a small smile. I knew she was really trying, and I wanted her to know that I appreciated the effort.

Anyway, I am not sure Coach is right about me coming out stronger or wiser, but I will come out different. For one thing, I will investigate whether I can write. It doesn't have to be Hannah-quality, but I bet I will have something interesting to say—and by that, I mean that I just might create something cool.

So after another long silence—this time to ten Mississippi—I said to Coach that I appreciated his belief in me, and I was going to go, but I would be back next week.

Then I said, "One more thing. This news about my dad will change me. I am just not sure how. I was thinking back to when we discussed humor—not that there is anything funny here. You said that there are creators and appreciators. That is true here too. My mom created a reaction in me, but at least right now, I don't appreciate it—at all! If I can't become an appreciator, I am going to ask for help."

Coach looked straight at me, twisting his hands in a way I hadn't seen. I wondered if it was the first time since I've known Coach that he wasn't quite sure what he wanted to say. He seemed to want to say something.

Finally, I heard, "Alfred, I am here, and I think you know that. But there is a bigger picture I want you to see. You will learn something about yourself in how you manage these uncomfortable feelings. Until now, I think you've never really had a major conflict with your mom. Conflicts like this build depth and a history that you will come to appreciate. You just can't see that right now."

I whispered, "I just hope I feel the same about my mom. She didn't need to keep the truth from me for so long."

"Well," Coach said, "To understand that we'd need to walk in her shoes. Some day you might understand, but not now. My guess? You will appreciate her differently and maybe even more. She has worked hard as a single mom and has led you with great instincts."

We were back to instincts—which I maybe have, but at that moment, all I could say for sure is that I had anger. That anger seemed to know its home, and it wasn't leaving.

So with that, I headed out. I was still confused, and the moody blues aren't fun. Coach, though, gave me some hope that this stage has an endpoint. I could probably google my way to some answers about the average length of time someone has the moody blues, but I am not going to do that. Instead, I am going to assume it's my time to get comfortable with the soft squishy bucket where emotions get placed.

Chunk 40:
A No-Goodbye Goodbye

*A*lfred has begun to let information about his dad settle in. Coach had been helpful in a quiet kind of way, but now Coach was heading out, and Alfred wanted to thank him and let Coach know that he was doing ok. The combination of Alfred's mom telling him to channel Glinda and find the power from within, and Coach telling Alfred he would find a new inner strength as he processed this discovery gave Alfred hope and made him feel almost comfortable. Alfred was now thinking about a few things he wanted to say to Coach before he departed.

Alfred: Hey, Coach. Thanks for finding the time. I know you are busy, so I thought about what specifically I wanted to cover. It comes in the form of one comment, one question, and one wish. I know I should have started out with, "How are you?" but I'm pretty sure I'm going to find out as we talk.

Coach: I like that—one comment, one question, and one wish.

That's very succinct.

Alfred: Ok, here goes. First, my comment. You taught me not to be a know-betterer. It's a great lesson — actually a trap that I can still fall into if I am not careful. But then I got to thinking that you are, in fact, a know-betterer but in a good way. You know so many things better than me, and it helps me that you do. So my comment is that at least in your role as Coach, being a know-betterer is a good thing. And you do it in a nice way. You usually ask me a question that gets me to where you want. My mom calls it "leading the horse to water" — though I know I'm not a horse.

Coach: I have to think about your comment, and no, you are definitely not a horse. I try to be helpful based on my years of experience working with people. The expression your mom used has a second part: "But you can't make him drink it," meaning you can't force a solution on someone. So thank you for what I think was a compliment, and I hope that if I am a know-betterer, I am a gentle one.

Alfred: It was definitely a compliment, and you are a gentle one.

Coach: One more thing. Please don't be thinking, "I can be a know-betterer like Coach if I'm careful," because if you do, I'd have to reject your high praise of me. That's because I wouldn't be leading by example, which we both know is very important.

Alfred: Ok. I will still pretend to know nothing. I've been doing it now for a whole year, and it almost comes naturally.

Coach: Great — well kind of. You know what I mean.

Chunk 40: A No-Goodbye Goodbye

Alfred: So now my question. When I met with my grandma, she told me that I should ask you about "resilience." We hadn't talked about that because, of course, we got sidelined with talk of my dad, but I need to come back to this. I promised her I would discuss resilience with you, and besides, it might be helpful to me sometime—providing I really understand it. I looked up the word in the dictionary, but I think my grandma gives it more meaning than Merriam Webster.

Coach: Yes, dictionaries can be on the dry side. Loosely speaking, resilience is about getting yourself up off the mat after you've been thrown down. Maybe a relationship hasn't worked out the way you'd hoped. Maybe something unfortunate has occurred with horrible consequences. What do you do to stay engaged in life? In baseball terms, how do you get yourself to the plate again for another pitch? If you're resilient, you find the strength to get to the plate.

Alfred: Got it. And now I know why my granny talked about it. She had a lot of sadness in her marriage to Grandpa, and just as they were about to try again, he up and died. Then she raised my mom by herself. So clearly, she needed resilience. By the way, your baseball analogies are getting better. This might be an area where I taught you something.

Coach: Definitely. You've taught me a lot. And not just about baseball and 5-tool players. We have Soho Globs, *Popposites*, and recently I learned about dogs and what their tail position means. Also, your grandma was right—we need to explore resilience, but we can leave that for next year.

Alfred: So I've given you one comment—about know better-ers. I asked one question—about resilience. And now I'll share my one wish.

Coach: Shoot.

Alfred: I didn't ask how you are because I think I know. You are sad that your mom isn't doing better. It's probably hard to look at the glass half full.

Coach: Alfred, you are spot on.

Alfred: So I wish for you that you find someone in your life who is as helpful to you as you are to me. Basically, I want a coach for my coach. There is only so much you can figure out on your own. Trust me. I'm smart, but I would never be where I am today without you. I call that "my big discovery."

Coach: Well, I am going to give that some thought. It's not always easy to find a voice you can hear and really listen to, but you've reminded me that I should try.

Alfred: And because I like ending on a happy note—a reminder that seeing the glass half full is always the best way to go—I have a surprise. Actually, I have two surprises for you.

Coach: I love happy surprises.

Alfred: My mom said "yes" to a puppy. My patience paid off. It was hard not to keep bringing it up, but then I heard my mom's frequent words—"Don't be a Johnny-one-note." Evidently, I can persist on a topic for longer than she'd like.

Coach: I love how you both got to "yes" on a puppy.

Alfred: We are getting a golden retriever. Joey helped me find a good breeder. The puppy is female, and her name will be Nellie.

Coach: How did you come up with Nellie?

Alfred: My mom had two requests. One was that we commit to training the puppy. In her words, "It will pay dividends." And the other is that we name her Nellie. She said that the reason wasn't that important, but it was her wish that I at least consider the name. I did better than that.

Coach: So, lots of progress has been made in a very short time.

Alfred: Hannah taught me that when you have your mind set on something, there's no point in waiting.

Coach: Congratulations. I am so happy for you. When I see you next, you will have to tell me about Nellie's early months. I know that between your capable mom, Joey's dog experience, and your dedication, all will be good.

Alfred: I just thought of another topic we should tackle next year, in addition to resilience: the power of can-do thinking. That's one more thing you bring to my world. And now for my second surprise. I baked you some Soho Globs, but I am hoping you will share them with your mom. Or maybe I should say they are for your mom, and I am hoping she will share them with you.

It's my small act of generosity, but you also know that Soho Globs are about as good as it gets.

Coach: Yes, they are about as good as it gets, and I thank you for your kindness. My mom thanks you too, and we will figure out how we divide up the spoils.

Alfred: Spoils?

Coach: "Spoils" does not mean "spoil" as in to go bad. In the context of how I used the word, it means "prize" or "loot." Alfred, in this case, your being literal made complete sense, even if it wasn't correct in terms of my word usage.

Alfred: Ok, thanks for one more small lesson. I am going to test my mom on the word and see if she knows it. She probably will. She's very smart. Anyway, I'm going to let you go now. I will be ok. I think you will be too—especially if you find a coach as good as mine. I'd start looking now, though. Again, to quote Hannah, "There's no point in waiting."

Coach: Thank you, Alfred. We'll stay in touch.

As is his custom, Coach stops in to say goodbye to Alfred's mom.

"I just had a great chat with Alfred. You made his day with Nellie, but even more, you have no idea how often he uses your words to guide him."

"Oh, so he said yes to 'Nellie'? I was hoping that would be our puppy's name, but I hadn't heard, and I left the decision to Alfred."

"Yes to Nellie. Maybe sometime you'll share what that name means to you."

"All in good time. Nellie will be healing on many levels. Alfred's and my recent conversation created a need for more healing, as you are well aware. I think we'll be ok, and I also knew that the day of dad-talk was coming. The irony is that after Alfred's and my painful conversation, I am now looking forward to the relief of Nellie as much as Alfred is."

"Well then, that's very good indeed. Healing together takes on extra significance. And on a different note, I want to thank you for your support, for giving me some creative ideas on how to connect with Alfred, and honestly, for being our meta-coach in the background. You've helped me and Alfred both — in ways you'll never know."

Alfred's mom is stunned silent, but the small tear down her cheek says more than any words she could utter.

Coach notices and can't help but ask, "You told me once that your mom refers to you as Ellie. Is it ok if I say, 'Goodbye Ellie. See you in the fall?'"

Ellie nods, "Yep, I'm good with that. Take care. Be strong for your mom."

Chunk 41:

A Good Walk Made Great

*C*oach and Hannah have left town, and Alfred is settling into the summer. With a new puppy, Alfred seeks Joey's company and dog-smarts. On most afternoons, the party of four goes for a walk to the park.

Joey: Alfred, you are really getting the hang of managing a puppy. Why Nellie even responds to her name.

Alfred: Well, I promised my mom I would take training seriously. And I see what a good dog Calvin is. So I'm basically trying to copy you. It helps that Nellie wants to please me. When I give her a command, I can tell she's trying to do what I ask. When I give her a treat and say, "good girl," her tail wags.

Joey: And I know you know this, but sometimes puppies just want to be puppies with no commands. They need a break—just like us. So make sure you take it easy.

Alfred: I know. I can tell by looking at her eyes when she's tired. I'm really not in a rush for Nellie to learn all her commands. We'll get there. I actually have another topic to discuss—even though I could talk dogs all day long with you.

Joey: Sure. Dogs are what I know best, but we can talk about anything.

Alfred: My topic is dog-related. You know how happy I am to have Nellie, don't you? But I think I'm having a hard time. I miss Hannah and Coach. I am still processing the identity of my dad. All I can say is, thank God I have you.

Joey: Alfred, you wouldn't expect Nellie to fill your dad's shoes—even if she does have two paws for each shoe. That was my attempt to be funny. You've said how humor helps everything.

Alfred: You were funny, and you even showed some math smarts.

Joey: Seriously, I think it's just another example of *Popposites*. You're super happy to have a puppy, and you miss two people who mean a lot to you, and one person whom you never met. I think you can miss someone you don't know because of stories you hear, or maybe the role in your life that they should have played. You have a lot of reasons to feel down.

Alfred: Not that I need reasons, right? I've learned that sometimes, you just are.

Joey: Sure. That's true. Anyway, I think your mom expected your mood to go south with Hannah and Coach not around. And maybe we can add a little bit of guilt that she didn't tell you about your dad sooner. So for all these reasons, maybe that's why she got you a puppy. Otherwise, maybe no Nellie.

Alfred: Joey, you size things up well. You are smart in a very practical way. Thank you for making sense out of everything. So now I have a different question: Do you ever get bored in the summer? Even though Calvin is great, don't you miss school a little?

Joey: Not one bit. I always have something to fill my time. I fix things. I go onto YouTube to see how things are made. I read about things I want to know something about, which is usually not the same as what our teachers want us to know about.

Alfred: For example?

Joey: Can you name an invention that happened during the civil war?

Alfred: No.

Joey: Neither could I. But then I read about it. Did you know that balloons were invented by a self-taught scientist—Thaddeus Lowe—and it was the first example of what they call "aerial reconnaissance," which is used in war. Lowe set up a balloon on the White House lawn and then went up in it. President Lincoln was so impressed that he sent him straight to the U.S. Army Balloon Corps.

Alfred: Are you teasing me?

Joey: I'm not. There really was this unit. The people in the balloons relayed information to the officers in the field using the telegraph, which had only been invented around fifteen years earlier. A lot was invented back then.

Alfred: Wow. I had no idea. This is what having freedom allows you to find. You identified inventions that we had absolutely no clue about.

Joey: Yes. I no longer care that I'm not great at math. I find my math skills when I need them—like when I'm building something. Then, I can measure and calculate with the best of them. But I care about my curiosity.

Alfred: You have just made me very curious. You've also helped me to see our summer very differently. Summer is going to equal freedom, plus Nellie.

Joey: Alfred, you are always the mathematician. Really—making an equation out of our summer experience? Anyway, come September, I will be doing what my teachers want—just not as well as you will. So that's why I appreciate summer. My mind gets to wander freely.

Alfred: All right. I'm going to think about topics that would be interesting to investigate. Maybe how cats are different than dogs? Or can anyone learn to sing on key? What led us to want to invent cars? What is the origin of the bicycle? And that's just a start. With my freedom, I can go anywhere. Suddenly, I am seeing blue sky all around—and green too, just like my mom. Joey, thank you.

Joey: Your welcome—but for what?

Alfred: For reminding me that our attitude matters most. Coach would call it "seeing the glass half full." And you've added a new twist by emphasizing curiosity.

Joey: If I've done all that, then I need to say, "thank you." I don't think that I'm deep like you are.

Alfred: I disagree. But right now, I've got you, Nellie, Calvin, and a mom who makes me Soho Globs, so I'm happy.

Joey: Sounds like you've got about everything.

Alfred: Well, almost, but we won't bring up Coach or Hannah or the dad that I never knew. Should we change things up tomorrow and head to a different park?

Joey: Sure.

Alfred: I'm warning you, though, that I'll probably come with thoughts on a topic I've researched.

Joey: Ok. Can we end our walk with a joke? We are kids, after all.

Alfred: Sure. Here's one. What kind of place should you never take a dog?

Joey: Too easy. The flea market. Try again.

Alfred: Ok. Here's one that's a play on words:

Knock, knock.

Who's there?

Defense.

Defense who?

Defense has a hole in it—that's how I got into your yard!

Joey: Much better. Ok, here's mine. How many dogs does it take to change a light bulb?

Alfred: Truly no idea.

Joey: Why change it? I can still pee on the carpet in the dark.

Alfred: Ok, my mom would not find that one funny.

Joey: Then share this one with your mom. Where do dogs go when they lose their tail? To the reTAIL store.

Alfred: Now that's a good one for my mom. Ok, gotta go. I have some thinking to do for tomorrow's walk. Thank you for putting me in a good mood. You aren't just a fixer of things, you know.

Joey: I know. See you tomorrow.

The Epilogue

Like most of Alfred's summers, this one began unscripted. Within weeks, though, Alfred's schedule took form, beginning with a morning walk with Nellie, Joey, and Calvin. With the help of Joey's "Chuckit!" launcher, Alfred could now throw the ball quite far for the dogs to chase. Joey had explained that "It's all about the lever, and we just made yours longer." Joey was like that—full of knowledge and explanations.

The summer also brought Alfred renewed comfort with his mom. Alfred's anger had lasted "long enough," he told himself. He decided that learning about his dad at the ripe age of fourteen was probably his mom's survival skill at play. She had resisted revisiting history and was doing her best just to raise him. From his time with Coach, Alfred knew that most people were "doing their best."

Alfred missed Coach but was working hard to re-hear Coach's words and behave in a way that would make Coach proud. He missed Hannah too, but he was betting she'd be back by the end of summer. So instead, he chose to focus on his spirited new puppy.

Alfred remained hopeful that he might have inherited his dad's writing genes. "It could happen," he told his mom. "After all, I inherited Grandma's math genes." His mom smiled. The thought of Alfred taking up writing made her happy. It could be Alfred's way to understand what he called "the soft squishy bucket of emotions" and teach her a thing or two as well.

Alfred's mom continued to worry about Alfred's summer. He'd had such a great school year, and she wanted life to remain positive for him. She had noticed Naruto wasn't doing it for Alfred, nor were Soho Globs, though he always remained appreciative. At least Nellie was a big morale boost.

From time to time, Alfred's mom would ask, "Alfred, how are you really doing?" Alfred would respond, "I am *really* doing fine," emphasizing "really." Alfred meant it. After all, he had a new puppy, an ever-growing friendship with Joey, and *The Big Bang Theory* series to watch. He also liked that he now had a 33% chance of beating his mom at chess.

Still, on one particularly quiet and aimless day, Alfred confessed, "I've told you that I am doing fine, and I am. But I do miss Coach, and I especially miss Hannah." Alfred's mom knew this, even before Alfred told her. After all, Hannah was Alfred's first true friend who challenged him in a way that no one else had. Her intelligence and commitment to things she cared about were easy to appreciate. Add to that the months they spent working together on *Popposites* — how could Alfred not miss Hannah?

But Alfred's mom, being a smart and intuitive presence in Alfred's life, had just the answer. "Why don't you email Hannah weekly with a substantial update on your summer? Use it to test out your writing skills. Maybe you will be like your dad. And writing Hannah will be a twofer or maybe even a threefer."

Alfred and his mom loved "twofers," where multiple benefits accrued from a single act. Alfred's mom went on to explain, "You will feel more connected and probably get some interesting updates from Hannah. You will start to document your unusual summer. And you will exercise your writing muscle."

Mom's comment about the writing muscle made Alfred smile. She was trying to add lightness and range to their communication. Alfred offered his own version of this. On one night, he surprised his mom upon her return from work with a trail of popcorn from the kitchen table to the sofa where a chessboard sat. Near the chessboard was a sign that read, "You have met your nemesis." Of course, before doing this, he checked with Joey, the expert on all things dogs related, to make sure it was safe, should Nellie eat a piece of popcorn.

The whole scene—popcorn, chess set, and Alfred's declarative note of superiority—made his mom laugh which, for Alfred, was the best of all.

Alfred proceeded to follow his mother's suggestion and emailed Hannah a "substantial" correspondence.

Hannah, this will catch you by surprise, I bet. I have an idea, though, or to be honest, my mom had an idea, and I thought it was a good one. I'd like to propose that we email each other weekly and share what we've been doing, what's on our minds, and anything interesting or funny that marked our day. That last phrase, "marked our day," is my attempt to add some style to my writing. How'd I do? Be honest. You always are. I am hoping that I inherited my dad's ability to write, but only time will tell. My emails to you will be the first test of this. If we are lucky, and it turns out that I can write as well as be the data-nerd that you know me to be, then maybe we can have some fun next year working on a sequel to Popposites. I have a small idea brewing. Spoiler alert.

The theme could center on the spirit of discovery. Whoa, look at me. "The spirit of discovery" might be a small indicator that I actually can write. I am pretty sure this theme comes from what I've experienced over the last year, but when I told my mom this, she said, and I quote, "The spirit of discovery is universal." That's good because it means that it's not all about me.

I hope you and Ben are well. I've been spending a lot of time with Joey, which has shown me how great he really is. I call him "My surprise inside the box of Cracker Jacks" because there is always something unexpected that he offers me. I wonder if the same might be true for you and Ben. You are siblings for life, so I am betting that it's going to work out just fine. It's all about that joy of discovery... oh the places we could go.

I am going to sign off in the best possible way—with a picture of Nellie. Boy, do I love her. My mom gave me a plaque that reads,

"Medicine heals the body. Dogs heal the soul."

I think it's true. And it sits right on my desk. Talk about inspiration!
Hope to hear from you soon.
Signed,
Your favorite data-nerd, and maybe your writing friend,
Alfred

How Alfred's Journey to Be Liked

Spoke to My Son and Me

By Scot Butwell

*W*hen I read *Alfred's Journey to Be Liked*, I had this unusual feeling, like it was written for my son. Not specifically, of course. But Alfred's challenges with social communication are similar to my son's and other neurodiverse kids in our world.

I know from what Ebstein has shared about her work that it was intended to be a "Social Bootcamp" as we exited the pandemic. We all lost some important social skills. Little did Ebstein know that she had created a neurodiverse boy—something she only learned of when she gave her book to friends, educators, and therapists to pre-read and comment on. The question she often heard was, "Who do you know who is autistic?" Ebstein and I connected because we both write on the social media site Medium, and when I read one of her stories about Alfred, I became immediately interested. If there was a tool to help my son's social skills, I wanted it.

As a parent of a fifteen-year-old autistic teenager, one of my main concerns is how to best help my son to develop his social skills. While Ebstein freely admits that she didn't set out to do so, she has written a book that can help parents like me engage with our children, inch by inch. It's probably why she refers to her chapters as "chunks" because progress will come in pieces, and at least from my experience, slowly. But the beauty of Alfred's journey is that we get an up-close view of those pieces—what I call "hidden social skills"—as he builds a more connected world.

Teaching social skills to a child is never easy—neurodiverse or not. You know kids … they're more likely to pick up a video game console than read a book. So just imagine the challenge of getting them to read a story focused on acquiring social skills. It's kind of like asking a teenager to clean up their room.

And yet, here's the thing I know from observing my son's life: Neurodiverse kids have a strong desire to have friends and to belong to a group. They may lack the skills or know-how, or attention span, but this doesn't eliminate their desire. It just tells us they need our support. Most people develop social skills intuitively as they grow older from experience. But for neurodiverse kids and adults, the process of developing these skills is not as natural.

My son went through a phase recently where his best friend became his frenemy. It was a very difficult situation, and I didn't know how to handle it. As I read Coach's social lessons, I see now that it was actually a great opportunity to talk about the social dynamics in the relationship. Of course, I wouldn't use those words, but I could refer to Coach's ideas in his lessons with Alfred as a way to talk to my son about the situation and to suggest possible solutions.

Some things I had to consider in the frenemy situation were, "What do you do when your friend is bossy and gives backhanded negative compliments?" I wondered how my son should react. Should he ignore his friend? End the friendship? Fight back with his choice of words? Should I be asking my son how he feels, helping him build some self-awareness? Having a shared experience of Alfred's journey would've been a helpful place to start a conversation, but this predated my reading Alfred's story. With a few simple questions and some of the lessons I've picked up from Coach, we could have been in a better place to deal with the frenemy problem.

One of Coach's lessons I like best is to look at ourselves and see what we bring to others. For example, how can we be generous toward others in a meaningful way, one that doesn't require resources? Coach helps Alfred see that giving of yourself is the best gift of all. Time. Patience. Support. Understanding. This type of generosity doesn't take a wallet. It only takes heart which is something my son has plenty of. His kind nature is a gift to everyone who knows him, and this is the lesson from Coach I've been emphasizing the most in talking with my son.

Coach uses baseball's "5-tool player" concept to help Alfred identify his strengths as a friend. In baseball, the five tools are hitting, hitting for power, running, fielding and throwing, but taken outside of baseball, the tools can mean anything. For Alfred, math, chess, and helping kids with homework are the core social tools he uses to interact with others. He is good at breaking things down into chunks. For my son, we are enjoying discussing his strengths as a friend by using baseball's five-tool model, and our list has already expanded to more than five tools.

Coach's lessons will take time to learn and apply. Another skill of Coach I like is to "hear the unspoken," but Alfred asks how we can hear things that don't make a sound. I love how Alfred is very literal, but he does learn that to "hear the unspoken" means to notice the body language of others. He learns that we all express our feelings with our tone of speech or slumped shoulders as much as with our words. No two neurodiverse kids are alike, and all are challenged socially in different ways, but Coach provides a roadmap with enough specificity and generalization where everyone can benefit.

Ebstein's novel has such a positive, can-do tone that I believe all readers will believe they can eventually get there. Like Alfred, we will get there if we "follow the breadcrumbs" (what Coach tells Alfred's mom), letting one social skill build on another. It's cool that we get to learn along with Alfred to pay attention to visual cues such as eye contact or to consider how a conversation is going. Does it roll along fluidly like a train at night, or does it start and stop? Is the conversation one-sided or two-sided? What is the person's body language like? Does the person seem interested or bored? Thinking about all these elements in a conversation helps Alfred to make a huge leap in his social understanding.

What I especially like about the book is that it's not all serious. There are many light-hearted moments that make for a fun read. My son and I loved reading about why "ha-ha matters," which is not surprising since humor is also one of my son's five tools. He loves to create funny YouTube videos. His latest video was telling his cousins he wanted to show them a video, and then I recorded their reaction to watching Rick Astley dancing. They had been "Rickrolled," a prank where a person clicks on a link and gets misdirected to a video of Astley's "Never Gonna Give You Up." It was the perfect example of how everyone has a role when it comes to humor. As Coach explains, there are both creators and appreciators who make laughter happen.

As a joint reading experience with my son, the best part was the short chapters—just five minutes or less, coupled with Alfred's "homework assignments" at the end. The chapters are mostly a dialogue between Coach and Alfred, so it goes fast. The parent in me appreciates that a conversation gets started that I might not have otherwise had with my son, and I get to use some fun vocabulary like "know-betterer" (Ebstein's term for a know-it-all) or "ha-ha" or "popposites" in talking about the subtle nuances of social skills.

I could go on about Coach's other lessons—ten in all—but I will leave you with how I felt after I finished Alfred's story. I realized I'd fallen in love with Alfred. Why? Because he reminded me of my son. Alfred is a quirky kid with a big heart who agrees to take on the challenge of improving his social skills at his mom's request. He doesn't really want to at first. He isn't convinced he needs to. But he loves his mom and wants to make her happy. Eventually, he tells her that she is right and his world is indeed better with more friends.

Alfred's story has become our story. My son and I are undergoing our own journey, and while we might not adopt all ten lessons, and we won't do it at lightning speed, we are on the path. With lessons from Coach and his interesting way of explaining social concepts, I feel I can help guide my son to develop the social skills he desires and handle the bumps on the road he encounters.

That's the gift of *Alfred's Journey to Be Liked.*

Alfred's Journey to Be Liked

Ten Simple Rules to Help Get Him There

*T*he following ten lessons are sprinkled throughout Alfred's journey. Still, for those who need to jump straight to the rules, I offer a brief summary. However, reading about how Alfred internalizes these lessons is a lesson in itself as he proceeds from an abstract rule to a new behavior. This is my pitch to actually read the book in its entirety.

Rule 1: Don't be a know-betterer (Chunk 2)

Definition: Coined by Coach, "know-betterer" describes the person who always thinks they know better than others. Expressions that convey a similar meaning are "smart aleck" and the snide observation that someone "thinks he is the smartest person in the room."

Application: Alfred tells Coach that when he meets someone, he asks what they enjoy, and then, if possible, Alfred responds with data about the particular interest. Alfred believes he is simply adding to the person's knowledge, not realizing it is off-putting.

Rule 2: Walk in someone's shoes (Chunk 3)

Definition: Try to understand your friends and family better by imagining what it's like to be them. What are their challenges? If you "walk in their shoes," you will build more empathy which is a key building block for a sustained friendship.

Application: Coach shares that one of his favorite books is *To Kill a Mockingbird*. Here, Atticus tells Scout, *"You never really understand a person until you consider things from his point of view... until you climb in his skin and walk around in it."*

Alfred, who is very literal in his understanding of the world, chooses to try on a friend's Converse sneakers to see what it feels like to run around on the basketball court and dribble a ball. Alfred proceeds from this literal interpretation to then explore his mom's and grandmother's past and his friends' current struggles.

Rule 3: Show generosity of spirit (Chunk 4)

Definition: Be generous in how you act and think. This requires kindness, not money. You put people at ease and communicate that you've got their back. This attitude is the truest and most important form of generosity.

Application: Alfred realizes that Hannah needs help with her play, *Popposites*. Even though he has no desire to be on stage and dislikes being the center of attention, he extends himself for the sake of their friendship. Alfred learns all the cast's lines so that, as narrator, he can give a prompt if needed. His generosity extends to subbing for a sick dancer, where his two left feet turn a serious dance into a feel-good comedy.

Rule 4: Ha-Ha matters (Chunk 6)

Definition: Use humor to add some fun and reduce the pressure of daily living. Humor helps build friendships because laughing together makes us what to spend more time together.

Application: When Alfred becomes the narrator for *Popposites*, he observes a very cranky cast. He is asked to become the "culture builder" and boost morale. He focuses on lifting the cast's mood by asking everyone to bring a joke. The humor lightens the mood.

Rule 5: Define and build your five tools (Chunk 14)

Definition: Everyone has strengths that can be built upon. Coach explains, "Tools equals confidence," and baseball's 5-tool player becomes an analogy that Alfred immediately understands. Knowing your five tools helps you be your best self and strongest friend. It also helps identify common interests among your peers and enables easier conversation.

Application: Alfred identifies his five tools as math, chess, teaching, making Soho Globs, and hearing the unspoken. He also identifies a sixth "aspirational" tool he intends to build—knowing which questions to ask and how to do so gently. This will later help in conversations with his mom.

Rule 6: Zigzags are a common occurrence in life (Chunk 8)

Definition: We seldom make continuous progress. Sometimes it's two steps forward and one step back. Understanding this universal experience will spare us disappointment when we backtrack. The path to friendships is a zigzag which enables us to better support our friends.

Application: Returning to school after winter break, Alfred finds his conversation with friends awkward. He wonders whether he has lost the emerging friendship skills. Coach explains the "zigzag," and from there, they find ways to facilitate Alfred's interactions. Alfred forms a chess club that plays to his passion. Most importantly, his expectations about progress are reset.

Rule 7: Face your fears (Chunk 9)

Definition: Often, our fears are nowhere near as bad as we imagine. Sometimes they amount to a hill of beans. By not running away, we can begin to understand and conquer our fears.

How does facing our fears help build friendships? We are more whole and healthy. We bring more to people as we radiate a positive attitude. What we radiate is radiated back.

Application: When Alfred worries that he has lost his conversation skills or that starting a chess club will be a flop, Coach explains that it is time to face his fears. Alfred proceeds with the club, albeit reluctantly. Many kids join, the outcome is positive, and Alfred's zigzag zags up.

Rule 8: Hear the unspoken (Chunk 15)

Definition: Focus on hearing what's on people's minds but unsaid. To hear the unspoken, we need to tune into some very soft signals—eye contact, body language, and the starts and stops of their speech. We need to depend upon our instincts and powers of observation. We must remember that what is not said is as important as what is.

Application:
Alfred makes "hearing the unspoken" one of his five personal tools. He uses it to read his mom, Joey, Hannah, and even Nellie, the puppy. He explains, "I need to consider whether what the person is saying makes any sense. Then look at the person and see if they are making eye contact… Then consider how I would feel if I were in their shoes."

Rule 9: Refresh, reset, timeout (Chunk 21)

Definition: It's as important to give yourself a break as it is to pursue a goal. We are not computers; we are people. We need to understand how to relax and recharge ourselves. Often referred to as "self-care," if we don't take care of ourselves, we are spent, and we will have nothing to offer others. Being watchful of our mood, "preventative maintenance" as applied to one's disposition, is critical in keeping us healthy and of sound mind.

Application: Between chess club, *Popposites*, and new friends, Alfred is irritable. When Coach suggests a "timeout to recharge," Alfred has his friends manage chess club. He takes a much-needed break, watches Naruto, eats Soho Globs, and finishes the night with a chess game with his mom. His battery is recharged.

Rule 10: Appreciate "popposites" as adding dimension to life (Chunk 18)

Definition: "Popposites" is a word that Alfred's friend, Hannah, invented. She uses it to show the tension and heightened beauty of opposites. For example, if you are traveling, the impending departure might yield anxiety, but the possibility of exploring new geographies yields excitement. As two sides of the same coin, both are real. How do popposites help with friendships? It helps build our tolerance for complexity. People have layers, and we can understand those layers better in a "popposites' state of mind."

Application: Alfred did not want to be Hannah's narrator, nor did he want to be Hannah's culture builder. As an act of loyalty, Alfred says "yes," and it forever changes how he sees the world. His internal resistance is balanced with his satisfaction at helping Hannah and the cast—"popposites" at work.

An Interview with Jill Ebstein

By Jill Ebstein

*N*ote: If Alfred can talk to himself and find out things, then Jill can too. Here goes.

Jill 1: Jill, it's time we answered a few questions about this unusual dialogue-mostly creation.

Jill 2: Ok, but I think it's odd that I have to interview myself.

Jill 1: Do you see anyone else standing in line to interview you? It's not odd. It's reality. Anyway, I've created a list of questions—almost like Hannah would do—and I'd like you to take a stab at giving your most honest answer.

Jill 2: You know me—which is really you know you. It's how I run. Let's go.

Question 1: Is Alfred "on the spectrum?" Or to use the more clinical term, "neurodivergent?"

Jill: I get asked this question all the time. I avoid labels because they are usually not helpful or accurate. I think we are all on the spectrum to varying degrees. Isn't that what the word "spectrum" implies? Having said that, therapists and friends who have read this book tell me that Alfred is not neurotypical, but there are ranges. He might be a high-performing neurodivergent character who doesn't quite click with conventional behavior. We know that he "runs very literal" and has a hard time interpreting the behaviors around him. We know that he is very smart and also very teachable. The Alfred that begins the book is not the Alfred who ends the book. The last three things I said is what I will stand by. The rest is for interpretation.

Question 2: Oh no! When you say, "ends the book," is this the end for Alfred and us?

Jill: Jill, you know that an end just marks the start of a new beginning, right? And so it is for Alfred. It's not our end or even Alfred's end. There is so much more for Alfred and his friends to explore. And by the way, we will get to explore that with him. Let not say more, though, for fear of spoilers.

Question 3: Why do you call the chapters "chunks?" It's going to seem crazy to the reader.

Jill: We chose chunks for a few reasons. The first is a belief that the way we solve complex problems is to break them down into chunks. Alfred is trying to solve the problem of how he can relate better to friends. There are many aspects to solving that. He is also trying to build a richer world while still providing the downtime he needs, which is another complex problem. With the help of Coach, he solves it bit by bit.

There is one other reason we opted for "chunks." This is an unusual book—between the dialogue format and how the book tells the story and reveals its characters. So, by using "chunk," we are signaling to the reader that this will be a bit different. We hope in a good way.

Question 4: Why is the book mostly dialogue?

Jill: There are a few reasons here. It's how I heard the story in my head. Also, I recognize the challenge of writing and being read when our attention spans are so short these days. I thought people would have a better chance of processing this story in a dialogue format. I begin and end most chunks with narrative to help set the stage and create context, but dialogue gives me a unique opportunity to highlight the play on words and move the story along quickly. Having said all that, I did add some traditional prose in terms of Alfred's voice by sharing some compositions he wrote. I hope for the best of both worlds—a speedy read and a strong feeling for Alfred by reading his work.

Question 5: Did you have a whole story in mind when you started the Alfred series?

Jill: The answer to that is a loud "No!" It just evolved. I would wake up and think to myself, "What would Alfred want to know about today? And how will it be teachable?" I realized I needed more characters for him to engage with, and then Alfred became the "thing" I thought about all the time. My poor family!

Question 6: Do you have a favorite character? Maybe someone who is like you, for example?

Jill: I love all the characters, truly. My introduction of Hannah caught be my surprise because I could see how easily I "got" her. Maybe I'm a little like her? I love the mom because she is smart, intuitive, and can control her boundaries. She gives Alfred lots of room to roam and is a quiet help to the Coach. You just know that she's been there. Joey is a shout-out to those students who weren't on the "honor roll" and were viewed as not "smart" but clearly are. Joey is smart in a different and very cool way, and his warmth and dependability are the best. Joey showed me an empathy in my writing that I didn't know I had.

In terms of who I think I'm like, I suspect that is a question most readers will ask themselves. Do I have some of Joey, or Alfred, or Hannah in me? I'd like to think that there is a piece of me in each character. I hope I am an intuitive mom who gives my kids room to explore. I hope I am organized, focused, and full of energy like Hannah. I hope I have Alfred's kindness and ability to learn and internalize those lessons. I hope I have Joey's helpfulness and auto-didactic ways. He learns best when he is on autopilot. I hope I have Coach's wisdom. It's one thing to write his script. It's another thing to believe and practice what he says.

Question 7: Do you have a favorite lesson that rose above all others?

Jill: The answer to that question is a another loud "NO." I don't have a favorite lesson because they're all important to me. However, there is one lesson that in our current environment, I use all the time and have incorporated into my vocabulary. "Don't be a know-betterer." We all have those tendencies which we need to contain. I am working on hearing others better and maintaining an open mind. We see how an open mind benefits Alfred and his mom in so many ways, culminating with Nellie.

Question 8: How did *Popposites* come into being, and why?

Jill: I needed a visual way to highlight life's complexity and show how two very opposing realities can be true. Not only that, but two opposing realities can add dimension and meaning to the other. I hope that if this idea makes it into a classroom, teachers can allow their students to explore the popposites in their life. *Popposites* provides so much room for creativity and connection. It might also help us not be know-betterers.

Question 9: Was there any moment in your story where you, as the writer, were particularly touched?

Jill: Lots of moments touched me as these characters seemed more real with each passing day. But the one moment that stands out is when Alfred tells his mom that he is fine and doesn't need a Coach. His mom responds that he is more than fine but could be even better. Those same words come back later when Alfred argues for a puppy, and his mom says that they are fine. I think we are often "fine," but better is well… better.

Question 10: Are you going to tell readers why Alfred's mom wanted the name "Nellie" for the puppy?

Jill: There is a story that will come out over time. In this case, time means sequels. There is still so much to learn. In the meantime, I hope readers exercise their imagination if they ponder the Nellie question.

Question 11: Was it hard to end the story?

Jill: As I said earlier, I don't believe that stories ever end. I hope I left the reader imagining the flow of the summer and the eventual return to school. We know that Alfred will come back changed in some way. Joey might return with a new recognition of what he brings to his world. Hannah is beginning the process of understanding how she can be happier. We know that success does not necessarily equal happiness.

As you know, we had twelve people read this book so that we could incorporate feedback or questions in the rewrite. The ending brought a significant source of questions for our readers. People did not want to say goodbye to Alfred. They wanted to know what would happen with Hannah as she begins to look inward. This felt like good news because people felt invested in the characters we created. In short, our work is not done.

Question 12: Do you love dogs? Is that why Calvin and Nellie make it into the book?

Jill: The short answer is yes. I love dogs. I also felt that given Joey's personality, a dog just felt right for him to have in his life.

Dogs, in some way, mimic what Joey brings to his world. They are instinctive and full of love. They "get us" with no words required. Joey, in the most unassuming and authentic of ways, is a tremendous source of support for Alfred. Joey, though, brings an added plus of curiosity and words to frame his world and enrich ours.

Question 13: Will there be a follow-on to *Alfred's Journey to Be Liked?*

Jill: There are, of course, many ways the story could extend itself. I will plead the fifth on this one. Time will tell— as in readers can check in come fall.

Question 14: Who do you think is the reader for this book? Young adults? Adults? Who??

Jill: As you know, we tested this because it didn't feel obvious. We found out that while teens might read this book, it requires more attention and probably offers less fun than, for example, speculative fiction or graphic novels. So while they might read it upon prompting, adults are the readers who really clicked with this book and had many, many questions.

So our short answer must be that adults are the primary readers but that they can read select sections with teens and engage in conversation. Can't we all benefit from not being know-betterers? Isn't it a relief to know that we can participate in humor as an appreciator? Who hasn't felt the clock being their master as we try to slow down the pace of our life? Who hasn't been like Dorothy in Wizard of Oz, realizing that power lies within ourselves? Who hasn't experienced anger that scatters itself into places it doesn't really belong? My hope is that adults will read this in support of the young adults in their lives, and it will facilitate conversation.

If adults and their teens can appreciate it together, it will be a twofer, which we know is best in the world of Alfred. I think we will also have to consider whether there is a companion book for younger readers that will be fun and have illustrations but that is a next-generation book. To be clear, though, we're not there yet. It sits as an idea.

Question 15: Is there any guidance we should particularly give our readers?

Jill: That's a great question, even if I asked it myself. Now that I've read this book a kazillion times, I will say that this is not a "binge-read," and it's better experienced when you read it in pieces. Then take a break. Then read some more. The goal of any reader should not be to speed-read it like it's a high-action thriller but rather to digest and consider each chunk before proceeding ahead. In this way, I think readers will get the most out of Alfred's journey.

Alfred's Journey to Be Liked

Study Guide Questions

1. Know-betterer: Coach explains to Alfred the importance of not being a know-betterer. Why does Coach think this is an important place for Alfred to start? Why do you think Alfred is a know-betterer? In what way does being a know-betterer get in the way of making friends?

2. Five Tools: Coach uses the 5-tool-analogy to help Alfred recognize his strengths. Alfred likes this idea so much he even writes a composition. Can you identify your five tools? Which of your tools currently exist and which are a work in progress? Does identifying your tools help you? If so, how?

3. Face your fears: There is a lot of talk about the importance of facing your fears. Alfred had to face his fears when he started chess club, and then again with *Popposites.* Have you had a "face your fears" kind of moment? How did you react? Does hindsight, and Alfred, make you think about that moment differently?

4. Popposites—where opposites pop: What is an example of a popposite in your life? Does seeing two things that are both connected and opposite add value in how you view them?

5. Challenging our assumptions: Coach asks Alfred to challenge some assumptions. For example, does data tell us the whole story? Alfred is intrigued by the "soft squishy bucket of emotions" that he hasn't paid much attention to, until maybe now. What are some assumptions in your life that you think are worth challenging?

6. Colors and entertainment: Do the shows we watch and the colors we are drawn to say something about us? Alfred and his mom talk a lot about colors. Alfred is relieved when he can add *The Big Bang Theory* to their evening experience versus *Friends*. Do you have a favorite series? Does your preference say something about you?

7. Float like a butterfly, sting like a bee: Do you have a style that you use for persuasion? Do different moments call for different styles? Is one style harder for you than the other?

8. Resilience: Granny makes a big deal about resilience. Why does she see this as so important? She says, "It's not how many times you get knocked down. It's how many times you get back up." Do you agree? Have you had moments where you've had to be resilient?

9. Humor: Coach describes creators and appreciators. Can one person be both? Are they equally important? How would you describe yourself?

10. When your anger does not know its home: Coach and Alfred discuss misplaced anger with regard to Hannah. It could also be applied later to Alfred when he learns of his dad. Explore the places Alfred could be angry and then where it shows up.

11. "Our mistakes are a laugh that we didn't plan for": Hannah repeats Alfred's idea and then uses it when she wants him to dance. Why did Alfred create this idea in the first place? How does this idea help the cast?

12. Culture builder: What do you think the role of a culture builder is? How can they help? What should they do in this role? Notice that it is "culture ***builder***" not "culture ***keeper***." Why?

13. Listening to the unspoken: This is high on Alfred's wish list and he works hard to develop these skills. Why does he care? Why does hearing the unspoken matter? Do Coach's tips help?

14. Alfred's mom and Glinda: Alfred's mom insists that they watch *Wizard of Oz* so that Alfred can internalize the lesson of "Click your heels three times" that Dorothy uses to get back to Kansas. What is Alfred's mom trying to show Alfred? Why is it important?

15. Coach: Not much is known about Coach other than he is a good listener, good son and calm presence who can connect to Alfred and his mom, and then later to Hannah. Is there a person who serves as "coach" in your life? If so, how is this person helpful?

16. Stuck in a hole: The prologue starts with a story from *West Wing* that Alfred's mom can't shake thinking about. This leads her to the idea of finding a coach to help Alfred. Alfred's mom is very intuitive and also thoughtful. Is "stuck in a hole" unusual or something that happens to everyone at one moment or another? The *West Wing* story ends with the friend who says, "I've been down here before, and I know the way out." Is that empathy? Being a know-betterer? Or something else?

The book ends with Alfred walking with Joey and their dogs, followed by a letter to Hannah. Why do you think the author chose to end the book this way?

If there were to be a sequel, what characters would you want to know more about? What stories feel incomplete?

Made in the USA
Middletown, DE
06 February 2023

23638389R00186